MYSTERY Magazine

FICTION

UP THE CHIMNEY HE ROSE
Gerard J Waggett 2

THE LAST DANCE OF DON DIEGO
John Kojak 19

THE GNOMES
A.M. Porter 27

CHARLIE'S WAR
John M. Floyd 36

CHANDLER IN THE CLASSROOM
Susan Oleksiw 50

NAUGHTY OR NICE
Michael Mallory 55

CHAIN OF HEARTS
J.T. Siemens 70

GINA'S GREATEST HITS
Lina Chern 78

FLEECE NAVIDAD
A You-Solve-It by Stacy Woodson 89

INQUIRIES & ADVERTISING

Address: Suite 22, 509 Commissioners Road West, London, Ontario, N6J 1Y5
Advertising: Email info@mysteryweekly.com
Editor: Kerry Carter **Publisher:** Chuck Carter **Cover Artist:** Robin Grenville-Evans
Submissions: https://mysteryweekly.com/submit.asp
Mystery Weekly Magazine is published monthly by AM Marketing Strategies. The stories in this magazine are all fictitious, and any resemblance between the characters in them and actual persons is completely coincidental. Reproduction or use, in any manner of editorial or pictorial content without express written permission is prohibited. Copyright on stories remain with the artist or author. No portion of this magazine or its cover may be reproduced without the artist's or author's permission.

UP THE CHIMNEY HE ROSE

Gerard J Waggett

My very first venture into amateur sleuthing, I unmasked the Santa Claus who surprised my third-grade class as none other than Mr. Blow, the school janitor! Jeannie Doyle broke down in tears, unable to handle the truth; the next day, during recess, her older brother punched me in the stomach. Undeterred, I collected evidence in the form of sales receipts proving that the presents left under the tree in our classroom had actually been bought by our own parents. Now, thirty years later, Santa Claus was sitting in my office, looking to hire a private investigator.

This was not the real Santa, mind you, but a far more convincing version than the 167-pound Mr. Blow. More than just heavy, this Santa (Gordon Nichols, "but call me Nick") was round, and his beard flowed off his chin and cheeks liked a gentle snowfall. I had met him two weeks ago while updating the security system at a mall. When he sat down at my table in the food court, I introduced myself as Timmy Gulliver, not Tim Gulliver, Tim*my*, which I had not gone by since well before high school. Nick asked me a bagful of questions about my work and was particularly impressed that my interest began with a junior detective kit I had received as a Christmas present. I suspected that he was looking to hire me, but I never could have guessed why.

Nick had shown up at my office in the red suit and without an appointment. When my assistant announced "Santa Claus is here to see you," I figured she was razzing me. All morning, she had been calling me Mr. Scrooge because I had limited the holiday decorations in my office to one single poinsettia plant, discreetly planted in the corner.

Right before Nick walked in, I had been hunting the Internet for a 3D video gaming console. The system my eight-year-old son Jake and every other kid in America wanted had sold out in the first two hours on Black Friday. Now the pirates of eBay had marked the price up five hundred percent. If the box wasn't sitting under the tree on Christmas morning, Jake would think he had done something wrong, or he might realize that there was no Santa Claus, but I could not justify paying upwards of a thousand dollars for a toy that would cost $250 in less than a month. My job here paid well, but not ridiculously well.

Since I was already on the computer, Nick directed me to look up Lester Manning in the town of Shaffer. Shaffer was located west of Boston, en route to the Berkshires. Lester Manning's family had earned its fortune in coal, which remained a popular source for heating homes in Shaffer and the surrounding towns. Lester Manning himself had been murdered in his own study two weeks ago. Someone had bludgeoned him with a brick from his own chimney. Even more curious, the study had been locked from the inside. The door had been latched shut, and the windows had not only been locked but caulked.

I had read about this murder. The story made national news primarily because of a joke the district attorney cracked. During a press conference, a reporter asked if the police were investigating the chimney as a possible means of escape. "Yes," the DA quipped, "we will be bringing Santa Claus in for questioning." Overnight, the Manning case became *The Santa Claus Murder*. Headlines were printed in red ink:

BAD SANTA

NAUGHTY SANTA

YOU BETTER WATCH OUT!

"Irresponsible." Nick was referring to the press coverage as well as the district attorney's comment. "Kids saw those headlines."

My own Jake had seen a promotional clip for a syndicated news program. The anchorwoman, if you could call her that, was asking, "Did Santa Claus commit murder?" The station had run the promo during their afternoon cartoons.

I had not followed the case after that first frenzy. Unlike Nick, I didn't have a vested interest. In addition to working at malls, Nick and his wife ran a Santa's Village not too far from Shaffer. Admissions this year had fallen off by nearly twenty percent. Mostly he blamed the economy, but he could not discount the effect of bad press. "I really don't care about the money," he said. "I modeled my life around this saint who loved children. I just cannot stomach seeing that image tarnished."

We both knew how the media operated. If nothing sensational happened in the next week, lazy reporters would dig up this murder, which had remained unsolved. Even with no new information, they would run an "update," probably on Christmas

Eve.

According to Nick, the sheriff in Shaffer suspected the wife. Sitting here in my office in downtown Boston, I suspected her as well. I had suspected the wife from the moment I read that Lester Manning had been survived by one.

"What are the three things the police need?" Nick took off his Santa's cap to think. "Motive is one of them. And they have a motive for the wife."

"Wives always have motive." In the twelve years we'd been together, I'd given my wife motive to kill me several times over.

Nick, who had recently celebrated his Golden Anniversary, admitted, "I have too."

"What have you done? Stay out all night?" I couldn't resist.

Nick had perfected his laugh. The "ho, ho, hos" boomed out of him.

"Means, motive and opportunity." That was the term he'd been looking for.

He could not differentiate between means and opportunity, but one of them pertained to the locked room in which Lester Manning had been found. If the police could not figure out how his wife had gotten herself out of the room, they could not place her in it at the time of the murder.

"That," Nick said, "is where I need your help."

"I don't investigate crimes anymore." In my mid-twenties, I opened up an agency with my roommate, a beefy guy who had played football in college. In my original business plan, we divided the work in half: I unraveled the mysteries, and Ben provided the muscle. Unlike me, he had them to provide. I was tall but lanky. The few times I likened myself to Sherlock Holmes, Ben reminded me that Sherlock Holmes knew how to box. Our business arrangement lasted only to the end of our six-month lease.

Nearly losing an eye showed me how completely unsuited I was for that business, especially for tailing people. At six four, I did not blend in with crowds. One unfaithful wife caught me snapping photos and pulled a knife out of her purse. I showed Nick the scar on my left cheek. My lucky scar—the wife *had* been aiming for my eye.

Nick winced in sympathy, "but I don't imagine Lydia Manning coming after you with a knife."

"What about a brick?" I patted the back of my head. My hair was dark brown and thick, but far from thick enough to cushion a blunt object.

"Maybe you could just look at the evidence," Nick said. "You might see something the police have missed."

"My buddy could do that for you." Ben's agency had grown into one of Boston's biggest. "And he won't charge half what we get here."

Nick frowned, and a cloud passed by, turning his beard momentarily grey. He had not flown here in a sleigh, he informed me. He had driven his Lexus and paid thirty dollars to park in the garage across the street. He understood that any company in a building with a concierge would charge premium rates. He would gladly pay those rates if I gave this case my best effort. After we chatted at the mall, he had Googled *Timmy Gulliver* and read a profile published in *Boston* magazine last year.

"You understand locations," he said.

That I did. I cased museums, hotels, jewelry stores, mansions ... I figured out every way an intruder could break in. Then I sat down and figured out a countermeasure for each of those ways. For someone raised in a God-fearing, law-abiding home, I had developed an uncanny knack for thinking like a professional thief.

"Can't you work that in reverse?" Nick asked. "Instead of thinking up ways to keep someone from getting in, can't you figure a way someone could have gotten out?"

The case did intrigue me. It intrigued me more than calculating the extra security details necessary for an upcoming boat show. Beyond that, my son Jake would never forgive me if I turned down Santa Claus.

Sheriff Peterson appreciated a fresh pair of eyes taking a look at the Manning case. (Unlike the district attorney, he refused to refer to it as The Santa Claus Murder.) The sheriff, who was in his mid-60s, wanted wrap up this case before he retired on New Year's Eve.

"Of course, Lydia did it," the sheriff said, but the locked room angle left the door open far too wide for reasonable doubt. Lydia Manning, who now had access to her husband's money, had already hired herself an A-list lawyer.

In addition to Manning's wife, a carpenter had been questioned in connection with the murder. Vern Cooper, an ex-con, had been working on the room in which Lester Manning was found dead. A van matching his had been spotted speeding away from the house the night Lester Manning was killed. His only alibi was a devoted wife, who swore on Baby Jesus that the two of them had spent the entire evening together watching Hallmark movies.

I would need to see the study where Lester Manning died, but I could envision a really gifted carpenter rigging some sort of door that could be latched from the outside.

Sheriff Peterson was chuckling but not at the theory itself. "Vern Cooper's not that bright. He's not even a very good carpenter."

"Then why would people who could afford the best hire him? Especially," I added, "given his criminal record. Any chance he and the wife ..."

The sheriff couldn't imagine Lydia Manning messing around with an ex-con, but even after forty years, Sheriff Peterson's in-laws still didn't understand what their baby sister saw in him.

Before I committed serious brainpower to this mystery, I needed to rule out some obvious possibilities. Number one, Lester Manning had not committed suicide. According to the coroner's report, the first blow to the head had knocked the man unconscious. The second one killed him. This also ruled out possibility number two, that Lester locked the door after the killer left. The unnecessary third blow to the mouth had probably been delivered to make some sort of statement.

Sheriff Peterson understood exactly the statement Lydia Manning had delivered: *Shut up once and for all*. Lester Manning had humiliated her for years. He not only pestered her about her weight, he snorted like a pig whenever she approached a dessert table. Sheriff Peterson had witnessed that for himself. Behind his wife's back but always so she could hear, Lester Manning pointed out all women he found smarter, thinner, prettier. But God forbid she refuse to attend some function. He would tell everyone she couldn't make it because she was "stuck home with diarrhea."

Sheriff Peterson never understood a man treating his wife like that. After his own wife lost her eyesight, the sheriff stopped cutting his hair. It had now grown back to the length it was when they first met. Of course, it was white now, not brown, but colors no longer mattered to his wife. She just liked running her fingers through his hair the way she remembered it feeling back then.

Officer Walter Galen knocked on the door. Just two years on the force, Officer Galen had discovered Lester Manning, his second dead body but his first murder victim. Officer Galen hit five-nine only thanks to a pair of thick-soled boots, but the twenty-three-year-old was solid. He shook my hand with gusto, excited to meet a private investigator. When he retired, he planned to open up his own agency.

"By the time you retire," the sheriff predicted, "you will want to get far far away from anything associated with crime." He himself planned to read classic novels to his wife and learn the piano.

The morning after Lester Manning had been killed, Officer Galen responded to a call Lydia Manning placed directly to the police station. When he showed up at the house, he did not realize he was walking into a murder scene. "I suspected suicide because she, Mrs. Manning, said that her husband locked himself in his den. Suicides go up dramatically this time of year." He had learned that fact in a criminal justice class at Shaffer Community College.

"I tried the door to the study, and it was locked. So I was knocking on the door, pounding on it, yelling, 'Mr. Manning! Mr. Manning! Are you all right! It's the police!' " Sheriff Peterson patted the air, and Officer Galen lowered his voice. "Mrs. Manning was getting very upset. She was crying and saying, 'He could be hurt. Just break the door down.' There was a long hallway, so I walked all the way down it and ran at the door with all my might." Despite his size, Walter had played football in high school. "He was lying there on the floor ... Mr. Manning. His face was all covered with blood, and there was a bloody brick not five feet away."

"Where was Mrs. Manning?" I asked.

"At the door. I had told her not to come in. She asked if he was dead. I told her I didn't know. I didn't want to say till I knew for sure. That's when I called you." He was talking to Sheriff Peterson, whose wife had not welcomed the intrusion upon their Sunday morning with the grandchildren.

Sheriff Peterson assured Walter, "You did the right thing calling me."

While Officer Galen was here, I needed to eliminate possibility number three: "There is no way that anyone was in that room when you broke into it? No one was hiding behind the door or in a closet ...?"

There was no closet in the room, and the officer had checked every corner.

"Was there anything odd about the room? Aside from the dead body on the floor," I added.

"Yes." Walter sat up in his chair. "There were six candles lit over by the door. The place just stunk of cinnamon."

"Cinnamon?" I asked.

Officer Galen could smell it the moment he walked in the front door. "I figured that Mrs. Manning had been baking."

Although Officer Galen wanted to stay, Sheriff Peterson sent him home to get some rest before his next shift. After he left, I hated asking, but I had to. "We can trust him?"

Sheriff Peterson nodded his head. "Implicitly."

The candles (which had almost definitely not been lit by Lester Manning himself) opened a few possibilities. "Any chance this was some sort of ritual slaying? Maybe a serial killer?"

The FBI had been called in. The one agent they sent didn't see any evidence for cult involvement. "They don't usually use holiday candles," he said. As for this being a serial killing, it didn't fit any pattern the agent had seen. Before he left, the agent told Sheriff Peterson, "The wife did it." How she got out of the room the FBI agent couldn't figure out, which made the sheriff feel like that much less of an idiot.

I moved onto obvious possibility number four: "There are no secret passageways or tunnels or trapdoors in that room, are there?"

The sheriff had studied the blueprints along with building plans and permits. He hadn't spotted anything suspicious, but I was welcome to take a look. I had taken a few architecture classes in college and a few more for my current job. As for the work Vern Cooper had been doing, the sheriff did not consider him capable of paneling walls much less installing secret panels.

"Before I forget," the sheriff added, "Walt took hundreds of digital photos in the den and all around the Manning house, inside and out. If you want to take a look at them, you can probably tell he would be thrilled to email them to you."

The photos could tell me something, but actually standing in that den would tell me more.

"How do I get in there?" I asked the sheriff.

He offered to call Lydia Manning on my behalf. "She's been surprisingly receptive to our visits. I think she's lonely."

The wreath that hung on the door with the red bows and gilded pinecones was far from funereal. Poinsettias flanked each of the front steps, and cranberry garlands wound their way up the wrought iron railings. From the bottom of the steps, with the front door closed, I could hear Elvis Presley's Christmas album playing inside.

Lydia Manning met me at the door with a plate of butter cookies sprinkled with red and green crystals. They smelled delicious, but I had never gone in for sweets.

"Don't worry. They're not poisoned." To prove it, she ate two.

Without a husband who'd complain, Lydia had stopped coloring her hair. Strands of silver now tinseled through the red.

"You really love Christmas …" I shouted over the music.

Lydia picked another cookie off the plate. "I always loved it, but then when it was taken away from me …"

"Taken away …?" I didn't need to ask by whom.

Lydia turned the music down but not off. "My husband believed that Christmas was for children. Since I hadn't given him any, which might have been his fault for all we know … Anyway, not having Christmas was my punishment for not having children."

I said, "It must have been hard living with someone like that."

She hadn't heard the sympathy in my voice as sincere. "If you're trying to goad me into a confession, it would not be admissible in court."

That I didn't know, but she had obviously researched this all very thoroughly.

Lester Manning's den had been left as it had been found several weeks ago. Yes, the dead body had been removed, but not the white tape with which the police had outlined it. The blood had yet to be cleaned up. You could see the stain on either side of the tape that had outlined Lester Manning's head. In spots, the blood blended in with the carpet, a maroon oriental.

The first of the year, Lydia would be throwing the rug out, gutting her husband's den and converting it into a gift-wrapping room. "That," she said, "will have Lester spinning in his grave."

The windows in the den had been shut, locked, and caulked since the first day of autumn. Lydia hadn't felt the need to air the room out. A faint hint of cinnamon hung in the air. I traced it over to two tables on either side of the door. A total of six jarred candles sat there, all of them large and all of them burned almost the entire way down to the bottom. I sniffed one and read the label: *Christmas Morning*.

Since Lydia would deny having done so herself, I asked, "Do you know any reason why your husband would have lit so many candles?"

"They say cinnamon's a popular scent with men." By *they*, she meant clerks at the candle shop. "Do you like it?"

"Well enough," certainly more than Walter Galen ever would again. "But so many candles in such a small area. Maybe your husband or his killer was trying to cover up some odor."

"What kind of odor?" Mrs. Manning sounded incensed.

My own wife hated insinuations that her house ever smelled of anything worse than apple pie and fresh cut roses.

I apologized and turned my attention to the door. According to Vern Cooper's invoice, he had stripped it and shellacked it to match the cherrywood mantelpiece. According to my eyes, the door did not match the mantlepiece.

Given the man's history and lack of talent, I had to ask, "Why did you hire Vern Cooper?"

Lydia Manning told me, "My husband hired him," but I didn't believe that. The Lester Manning Sheriff Peterson described did not support second chances for convicted felons.

"Did your husband know about Vern's prison record?" I asked. "Did he know he'd been convicted of breaking into homes?"

"Vern didn't charge much, and my husband could be a bit of a Scrooge." She was lying again, maybe not about her husband but about Vern Cooper. Despite the poor quality of work he delivered, he charged above union rates.

Her body stiffened when I touched the four holes Vern had drilled into the doorframe. My middle fingertip glided over each one as if reading Braille. The anchor mount for the latch lock had been screwed into the door right above the knob. The other mount Vern had screwed to the doorframe. When Officer Galen busted in here, the force yanked the second mount out of the doorframe, screws and all. It propelled the frame across the room and scattered the screws across the floor.

Somehow, that same force also ripped out a chunk of the door jamb. I stuck the tip of my finger into the little crater that had been created. The ragged wood inside it felt like fur.

"Are you almost done?" The impatience in Lydia Manning's voice told me that I was getting hot if not scalding.

I stepped back and checked the door. The anchor mount was still attached, but only loosely. "I assume the latch was your husband's idea."

"He valued his privacy."

"So he wasn't afraid of you."

"No, he was not afraid of me." Lydia said this with an air of disappointment.

"What about you? Were you afraid of him?" My firm had installed security systems in various shelters for battered women. Physical violence, I'd learned, often started off with the sort of verbal abuse to which Lester Manning had long subjected his wife.

"I wish he had hit me," she said. "That would have pushed me to leave."

Not knowing how to respond to a statement like that, I promised her that I was almost done. Before I left, I needed to satisfy my curiosity. I squatted down in front of the fireplace and pulled a tape measure out of my back pocket. No, Lydia Manning could not have squeezed herself up that chimney. No one could.

"The District Attorney accused Santa Claus of killing my husband. Isn't that funny?" Lydia had not only stepped into the den, she had crept right up behind me.

Lydia Manning standing that close to the back of my head made the hairs stand on end. I hopped to my feet and turned around.

"People are joking about Lester's death all over town and on the news." That brought a smile to her face. "You wouldn't believe the crude jokes he made at my mother's funeral."

A metallic green garland hung from one wall in uneven scallops, the bar's only acknowledgment of the holiday season. After limiting the decorations in my office to one ostracized poinsettia, I couldn't exactly criticize.

My wife would flip out if she knew I had walked into a dive like this, even at two o'clock in the afternoon, without police protection. She would stroke my scar, her fingernail perilously and intentionally close to my left eye. "You have beautiful brown eyes," she'd tell me. "I like looking into them. Both of them."

I had not planned to question Vern Cooper without Sheriff Peterson or Walter Galen, but the man was running late, and I was feeling a tad invincible. All by my lonesome, I had interrogated and survived Lydia Manning, murderess.

Vern Cooper was sitting at the far end of the bar, scratching a lottery ticket with his thumbnail. Since his most recent mug shot, he had shaved off all his hair. (More than likely, he had not sold it to buy his wife a Christmas present.) The four dollars he won off his scratch ticket bought him another beer.

I left one empty stool between us. "You're Vern Cooper, aren't you?"

"Nope."

"If you were," I said, "Lydia Manning wanted me to say hi."

Vern put down his mug. "How do you know her?"

"I'm thinking about buying her house." My old partner Ben complained that I enjoyed role-playing a little too much. He also vetoed my proposal to invest any of our start-up capital into a theater-quality make-up kit.

Vern didn't seem surprised that Lydia Manning might be selling her house. "If I was her, I wouldn't still be sticking around."

"Why not?" I waited a moment for him to answer, then moved on. "I'm looking for a carpenter."

This was turning out to be Vern Cooper's lucky day. First, he quadrupled his bet on a dollar scratch ticket. Now someone was offering him a job—and a beer.

"Lydia Manning showed me the study you fixed up. Nice work. Who hired you to do it? Her or her husband?" To me, it sounded like a reasonable question from a potential employer.

His response summed up the whole reason why he was sitting at a bar and not working on a Tuesday afternoon. "What difference does that make?"

"In case I need a reference ..."

"Ask Lydia Manning. She'll tell you how good I am." He sounded very confident.

"So *she* was the one who hired you?"

Vern didn't answer. Nor did he thank me for the beer.

"I'm thinking about replacing the lock on the door to the den. A little privacy from the wife." I flashed him my wedding band. "What would you recommend?"

"Dead bolt."

"But you only put a latch lock on the den in the Manning house."

Vern said, "That's all she wanted."

Bingo! "Did you say 'she?'"

Vern stared at the beer in front of me, which I had not yet even sipped. "Are you some reporter?"

"No." I threw a five-dollar bill onto the stretch of bar between Vern and me. "Next round's my treat."

I made my way quickly but not running toward the door. As I passed by the table nearest the front door, the two women sitting there were staring behind me. I knew what they were looking at. I knew Vern was following me. Despite his career in burglary, he hadn't exactly mastered stealth. His work boots hammered against the linoleum.

The right boot kicked my car door shut the second I had opened it. If I hadn't pulled my hand away, I might have lost a thumb. In case his foot hadn't done enough damage, Vern then threw me against the door.

"Who are you?" Vern raised his hand, the tip of his thumb completely grey. With the boots, he was tall enough to make contact with my face. He would have thrown that punch too if not for the wail of the police siren.

The second Sheriff Peterson stepped out of his car, Vern pointed at me. "He started it."

The sheriff smiled, a surprisingly soft smile under the circumstances. "Started what, Vern?"

"They'll back me up." Vern was now pointing to the bartender and two women, standing in the doorway watching. When the sheriff asked if I was all right, Vern answered for me. "He's fine. He's a reporter."

"Actually," I said, "the door handle slammed into my coccyx."

The sheriff translated for Vern: "Tailbone." He also identified me as someone working with him.

"He didn't say so. He said he was buying Lydia Manning's house. That's entrapment." Vern knew his rights.

Sheriff Peterson didn't bother explaining the actual laws governing entrapment. He merely pointed out that throwing me against my car constituted battery, which violated the terms of his parole. This prompted a rapid string of obscenities, one of them aimed at Lydia Manning.

While the sheriff loaded a handcuffed Vern into the backseat of the police car, I tried opening the driver's side door of my own car. The key unlocked it. Through the window I could see the button pop up. I just couldn't pull the door open. I tugged at the handle three times, the last using both hands. At that point, the sheriff called a tow truck and drove me back to the station. A now very accommodating Vern was telling me about a mechanic friend of his who would fix my door for free.

Faced with the possibility of heading back to prison, Vern finally admitted to being at the Manning house the night Lester Manning died. He also answered my questions for the record: Lester Manning had not hired him. Lydia Manning had. She hired him to strip and shellac the door, winterize the windows and install the latch.

As Vern confirmed the details I already knew, I kept thinking about my car door, which I needed fixed before Nancy saw it. No way, however, would I be trusting the car to any friend of Vern Cooper's. The dent his boot left made me think of the chunk missing from the door jamb in Lester Manning's study. I had almost connected the two when Vern started shouting, "That's not fair! You can't do that!"

The sheriff was threatening to arrest Vern's wife. By admitting that he had gone to the Manning house, Vern had just exposed the alibi as a lie. Providing a false alibi was a crime, which Vern knew all too well. He'd been arrested for it twice.

"Without someone to bail her out," the sheriff said, "your wife might be spending Christmas behind bars."

No one in her family would bail the poor woman out. They had disowned her during Vern's last stint in prison. "Come on, Sheriff," Vern said, "*Your* wife woulda done the same."

Sheriff Peterson never discussed his wife with criminals; he wouldn't even mention her name in front of them. "Maybe neither of you have to go to jail. Maybe you could just tell us what happened at the Manning house?"

To protect his wife, Vern would write it all down. "But I don't know if you're going to believe me."

The sheriff promised to keep an open mind. "Just don't tell me Santa Claus killed Lester Manning."

Officer Galen had not set foot inside the Manning house since the day after he discovered the body. It took Lydia a moment to place his face. As soon as she did, she cupped her hands around it and told him, "It's so good to see you again."

Tonight, the music was loud, but not blaring. I couldn't identify the woman singing, but the cover to Peggy Lee's *Christmas Carousel* was propped up on top of the stereo. The Yule logs added a cedar musk to the living room's almost overwhelming scent of pine. So far, Lydia Manning had only trimmed the bottom half of the ten-foot tree. Because of my height, she was hoping I'd hang the ornaments that needed to go on the upper branches.

The eggnog she offered had been spiked with "nothing worse than rum." She had been drinking it all day. She finished off the cup she was holding, licked her lips and refilled.

"Lester, I wish you could see me now." She was speaking to the flames in the fireplace.

Midway through the song "Happy Holidays" (which I did recognize,) Sheriff Peterson lifted the needle. "This is serious," he told Lydia and handed her a photocopy of Vern Cooper's statement …

Last Christmas Eve I went to the Manning House. I showed up there just before 9:00 at night. Mrs. Lydia Manning called me over because she said she had a necklace she thought I'd like to give to my wife.

When I got there, she asked me to wait in the front hall while she fetched the necklace from the safe. A couple minutes later I heard her screaming. The sound was coming from the study. When I got there the door was shut + locked. I screamed through the door a couple times, asking her to open up, but she just kept screaming Help! Help! So I backed up a few steps + threw my weight aganst the door. It busted open.

Mrs. Manning was standing by the fireplace. Her husband was lying face down on the floor, blood was oozing out of his head. There was a brick next to his head.

I asked "What happened?"

Mrs. Manning said "Somebody killed my husband." She was no longer screaming. Actually she was talking pretty calm.

I said we needed to call the police.

"Theyll think you did it" she told me. "Theyll think you came here to rob us. Theyll think you forced me to open the safe, then you killed my husband." She pointed to a wall safe that was opened up.

I told her "Tell them I didn't do it"

"No, I won't" she said. "If I tell them that, they'll think I did it."

Thats when it hit me maybe she was the one who killed her husband. The room was locked and there was nobody else in there with her.

"Who do you think they'll believe?" she asked me. "An ex-convict with a history

braking into houses or me?"

I knew who theyd believe. And I couldnt afford a lawyers who'd make anyone think different.

Then she told me she had a solution. A way nobody had to go to jail. I asked her what it was but she wouldnt tell me. She just told me that it was important for me never to tell anyone what I seen that night. Not even my wife. Dont tell anybody I was even there + I had to go home right then. So I did.

Lydia handed Vern's statement back to Sheriff Peterson. Eventually, she realized, Vern would tell the police what he had seen. She had already prepared her response; she probably prepared it before she even summoned him to the house: "If Vern Cooper was here that night, he killed Lester. I warned Lester not to hire an ex-convict, but you can't tell my husband anything."

As much as the sheriff hated to contradict a lady, "Vern told us you hired him."

"He's lying. You've already caught him in one lie. He and his wife said they were home all night. Now," Lydia said, "he claims he was here."

Before coming over, the sheriff had checked Lydia's phone records.

She *had* called Vern Cooper's cell phone at 8:07 that night. The call lasted four minutes.

She did not deny calling him. "But I wasn't going to give him a necklace. I called about work I wanted to hire him for."

"What kind of work?" the sheriff asked.

"Just little projects around the house," she replied.

I took another look at the ten-foot tree and the woman's sweater covered with red and green sequins. However many Christmases had been forbidden in the past, Lydia Manning was making up for them.

"If Vern came here that night," she said, "he obviously came here to rob us. Either Lester wouldn't cooperate, or he said something to tick Vern off. My husband was very good at that."

Sheriff Peterson could not contradict her there.

"What did he say?" I asked.

"I wouldn't know," she replied. "I was upstairs—"

"—listening to Christmas music." By this point, the sheriff had memorized her statement.

While Lydia preferred playing the classics like Peggy Lee and Bing Crosby on a record player, she had bought an iPod, a present to herself, for the express purpose of listening to music in secret.

"Now would you mind putting the music back on. And flip the record over." Lydia reached into the cardboard box which was sitting on top of the couch. She pulled out an ornament, a porcelain elf, and handed it to Officer Galen—who was no longer there.

"Where's that young man?" she asked.

"He wanted to check out the den," I replied.

"That's rude." She hung the ornament off the side of the box. "You don't go roaming around someone's house without permission."

Sheriff Peterson and I followed Lydia down the hall. The door to her husband's den was shut and apparently locked as well. Her left hand was twisting the knob and pushing in while her right hand slapped at the wood.

"What's he doing in there?" she demanded. "And why did he lock the door?"

"Is it actually locked?" I asked.

"You try," she said and stepped out of the way.

With my middle knuckle I rapped on the door: knock-knock-knock … knock-knock-knock … knock-knock-*knock* … knockknock ("Jingle Bells".) Like magic, the door opened. Officer Galen, my assistant for this little trick, stood there glowing, candles lit on either side of him. Per my instructions, he had been leaning all his weight against the other side of the door.

"Just because a door can't open doesn't mean it's locked." I told Lydia all about Vern jamming my car door shut. "That got me thinking, maybe when Officer Galen arrived here that morning, the door wasn't locked."

"It felt locked," Officer Galen said.

"It might have felt locked if it had swelled the way some doors do in the summer. Or if," I added, "it had been glued shut."

I tapped at the crater halfway up the doorjamb. Only Officer Galen leaned down to see what I was touching. "I did that," he said.

"Because the door had been glued to the jamb," I told him.

"Take the door," Lydia told us. "Take it as my gift. Take it to your police lab and let them examine it for glue."

"They won't find any." I'd already told the sheriff that. "You were too smart to use glue."

In spite of the circumstances, Lydia smiled at the compliment. Her late husband had never called her smart.

"You need something that worked like glue but wouldn't raise suspicion if the police did analyze the door. Something like ..." I held out my hand to Officer Galen, who placed a small can of shellac in it. "Spread a coat right about here ..." I tapped the can right above the knob. "... shut the door, and the next morning, good as locked."

"The only trouble with shellac ..." I peeled the lid up, and the smell immediately hit us all.

"That's why she needed the candles." Officer Galen had taken great pride in figuring that out on his own.

"Six of those candles together would drown out any scent of shellac still lingering the next morning." I resealed the can before the smell made me nauseous. "The heat from the candles also helped the shellac dry faster."

"I want you all to leave." Lydia was now raising her voice. "If I need to, I will call my lawyer."

"You will need to call your lawyer."

While Lydia stood there, absorbing the sheriff's comment, I continued. Because Officer Galen was now hanging on my every word, I directed my explanation toward him. "After Vern Cooper busted in the door, Lydia shellacked the inner frame and pulled the door shut. The next morning, when she came down—"

Not tall enough to reach the back of my head with any force, Lydia slapped me across the shoulder blade. "Stop talking about me like I'm not right behind you!"

The sheriff grabbed her wrist. "Easy, Lydia."

"Should I continue?" I asked him.

"Definitely, but Lydia has a point." He spoke in that tone of his that could calm grizzlies down. "Let's not talk about her like she's not here. This *is* her house."

I turned so that I was now facing all three of them. "When Officer Galen here busted in the door, he assumed he was the one who had broken the latch. He assumed that whatever damage had been done to the door—"

"It never occurred to me—"

"Me either," the sheriff assured the young officer.

"It was a brilliant plan." I owed Lydia that. "Your one big mistake, you didn't pick the best accomplice. But you needed him kind of dumb."

Officer Galen asked, "Why'd she need him at all? Why not just break down the door herself?"

Not wanting to be accused of excluding our hostess from the conversation, I offered her the first chance to answer Officer Galen's question. When she just turned her head, I explained, "She probably knew she couldn't break it in, not without hurting herself."

She did not contradict me.

Sheriff Peterson pulled out his handcuffs. "Lydia Manning, you are under arrest for suspicion of murder in the first degree."

Before he could begin reciting her rights, she warned him, "You know you'll look like a fool. You spend weeks trying to solve a murder, and this private investigator half your age comes up from Boston and figures it out in one day."

"I couldn't have done that," I said, "without all the work he'd put in."

Lydia ignored my comment. "They'll think you're getting old."

"I am getting old," he admitted.

"And senile. To miss all you did, people will think you must be going blind." Along with the house and the fortune, Lydia had also inherited her late husband's vicious tongue.

The District Attorney did not fight Lydia Manning's petition for bail. Nor did she request some astronomical figure. Sheriff Peterson did not believe that any holiday spirit had tripled the size of the district's attorney's heart. No, the DA was hoping that Lydia would flee the country never to be seen again. My shellac theory sold newspapers, but whether a jury would buy it remained to be seen.

Nick did not begrudge Lydia one last Christmas at home, especially after hearing about all the ones that had been denied her. Despite his busy schedule, he stopped by my house Christmas Eve to drop off a present for Jake. "The least I can do," Nick called it after I convinced my bosses not to charge him so much as a ha'penny.

"We couldn't buy the sort of press this case had generated," I mentioned, and they agreed. I had been quoted in a dozen papers, a couple of them national. Nick had brought along a copy of *The Boston Herald* for me to autograph. *SANTA CLEARED* the headline read. The illustration of Santa Claus underneath it could not have looked more like Nick if he had posed for the artist.

Jake thought so too. By age eight, I had already disproved the existence of Santa Claus to my classmates and brothers, but Jake still believed. If he had been harboring any suspicions, five minutes with Nick dispelled them. Nick nearly restored my own belief when he opened his bag and pulled out a 3D video game system.

How he knew Jake wanted it I didn't need to ask. Every kid who sat on Santa's lap this last month asked for one. But how Nick had gotten hold of one, and how he knew I hadn't, and for that matter how he knew where I lived …

Nick laid his finger aside of his nose. "Timmy, turn around for a minute, so we can pretend I left through the chimney."

THE LAST DANCE OF DON DIEGO

John Kojak

My name is María, and when I was fourteen I witnessed a murder. I still remember everything about that day. It began, like most days, with the feral heat of the rising sun upon my back as I labored through my morning chores, and the bitter words of my parents buzzing in my ears like angry bees.

Most days were difficult, but I knew this day would be especially bad. Don Diego, the wealthy owner of a silver mine in the hills above our town, had decided to throw a lavish fiesta in honor of his birthday. Our town was poor, so most people saw it as an act of generosity, but not my father. He hated Don Diego.

"Fiesta? For what?" my father seethed. "That chingado? Who is he? He is nothing."

"Be quite you old fool. Look at you. You are the one who is nothing," my mother replied.

"I forbid you to go! This family takes nothing from that man."

"If you worked, if you still gave a damn about providing for this family, maybe we wouldn't have to."

"I work …" my father said as he raised another cup of liquor to his lips.

"Really?"

"I work every day to restore this families honor!" He slammed the empty wooden cup down on the table and it went careening to the floor.

"Ha!" my mother scoffed. "A drunk, that is what you are."

As my mother stewed and my father drank, I rushed through my chores and started to get ready. I could barely conceal my excitement as I put on my colorful red and white cotton dress and the black leather shoes. The smells of roasted pig, chicken, and a thousand spices had been swirling in the wind since dawn. My only worry was that I might suddenly die before getting a chance to eat any of it.

Just after noon my mother rapped on my bedroom door. "Mija, hurry up. It's almost time to go. I want to get there before all the good food is eaten."

By then my father had finished his first bottle of pulque, the cheap milky-white liquor made from the fermented sap of agave plants, and his vitriol had boiled over into a sea of venom. "He thinks he can buy this town with his food … Ha! I hope he chokes on it. Now that would be something to celebrate!"

My mother had heard it all before. "Come, María. Let's leave your father to his sins." She made the sign of the cross and whispered a prayer—or it might have been a curse—before she grabbed me by the hand and whisked me out the door. She dragged me up the hill to town like a dog on a leash, complaining the whole way about my father, "I hate that you have to see your father like this. He used to be a good man, a proud man, but he has not been the same since we lost our land. Now all he does is drink and rail against Don Diego. You mustn't ever dwell on these things, María, the past is the past."

I wished my father could forget the past, but I knew that would never happen. For him, the past was an idyllic place where he was the respected owner of a large and prosperous hacienda, and Diego Rivera—Don Diego—was a poor peon who worked our fields alongside his father. The land had been in my family for generations … but then the drought came. It did not rain in our valley for many years. I was a small child when it began, but people say it was so dry that even the scorpions turned to dust. With the soil barren, my father was forced to let his workers go. Diego's father was said to be so distraught with the loss of our family's patronage that he dropped dead when he heard the news. It was not known what happened to the son after that … not until much later.

After several years with no rain, my father had no choice but to sell our land. Some said it was a miracle that anyone bought it. The entire valley was nothing but scorched earth, but a lawyer representing a mysterious buyer soon appeared and purchased the once proud and thriving hacienda for a few thousand meager pesos. What my father didn't know when he sold our land and, what he could have never imagined, was that the mysterious buyer was Diego Rivera. My father never got over the shame that Diego, the once destitute son of a peon, was now the owner of our family's legacy—he would never forgive him for that.

Diego Rivera's sudden wealth, and the noble title of Don that accompanied it, came from silver. How he discovered the silver was a great mystery, but he was now one of the wealthiest men in the state of Nuevo León.

But none of that mattered today, at least not to me. As we entered the plaza my mother and I were both overcome with joy. Everyone I had ever met was there, and many more. There were musicians, people dancing, and every kind of food you could imagine: pork, chicken, tamales, tortillas, chilies, frijoles, empanadas, churros, and lots of candy! I ate, and ate, and danced, and ate.

I was having the time of my young life, it was like my birthday, Christmas, and Easter all rolled into one. The only thing missing was my father. As the sun went down, the thought of him drinking alone, with only stale bread and beans to fill his stomach, filled my heart with sadness. So once it got dark, I wrapped a few tamales in a small piece of cloth and snuck away from the Fiesta. I thought if I hurried, and took a shortcut down a small arroyo behind the church, I could be back before my mother realized I was missing.

My father would never accept anything he *knew* came from Don Diego's table, but I thought that if I left the tamales on an open windowsill the aroma of masa and pork would waft into the room where he was drinking. If he had not passed out by then, I was sure that he would eat them. The thought of my father being happy, if only for a moment, delighted me, and I was running in a full sprint when I heard the scream.

I slid to stop in the loose gravel and looked over my shoulder toward the back of the church. To my surprise I saw Don Diego stumble out of the shadows and into the moonlight. A man that I had never seen before, wearing a large sombrero and black leather chaps with silver conches, followed and they quickly embraced, like dancers, with their right arms held out high above their heads and their left arms clinging to the others waist. They moved backward and forward, each seeming to take the lead, as they twisted and twirled across the rocky terrain. Suddenly, there was a flash of steel, followed by a shrill shriek, and Don Diego stumbled backward and collapsed to the ground. The man in the sombrero stood above him for moment, and then disappeared back into the shadows.

I stared at Don Diego's lifeless body for several moments until a bolt of panic swept through me. I dropped the food and ran home, leaping over rocks and brush like a fox, until I breathlessly burst through the door. My father hadn't moved. He was sitting at the small wooden table near the fire, his chin on his chest and an empty bottle of Pulque laying on its side in front of him. I frantically tried to wake him and tell him what I had seen, but he was too drunk to understand what I was saying. Desperate, I ran back toward town to tell my mother, but by then a large crowd had gathered around the body of Don Diego. Everyone in town knew how much my father hated Don Diego, and I heard several men shouting that he must have been the one who killed him. I was frantic, and must have looked like a chicken running around after its head is cut off as I turned again and ran back to warn my father. I was yelling at the top of my lungs and slapping his head and shoulders, but I could not wake him before an angry group of men burst into our house and dragged him off so fast that I could not tell them what I had seen.

I could hear my mother sobbing outside. I ran to her and told her what I had witnessed, but she was too hysterical to listen. No one would listen!

Even if they did, I knew they wouldn't believe me. No one would believe a girl. If I wanted to save my father, I would have to find the man who killed Don Diego myself. I did not know who he was, but I had seen men dressed in sombreros and leather chaps before, they were vaqueros—cowboys.

I had heard men talk of a cattle trail north of town that ran along the edge of the foothills to the river, and then through the pass to Monterrey. While everyone was distracted by the mob that had gathered outside our home, I crept over to our neighbor's barn and led a short-legged grey mule called Chaparrita out into darkness.

I rode Chaparrita through the night, with no real idea of where I was going, only the general direction of the river.

As the sun rose, my weary eyes began to distinguish the dark forms of cattle in the distance. Somehow, I had found them. I could smell beans and pork belly cooking over distant fires and hear the voices of crude men beginning their day with insults and stories of each other's wives.

Suddenly a rider appeared over a ridge in front of me. It was him! I did not get a good look at his face that night, but I would never forget the fancy black leather chaps with silver conches running up their sides. As he rode quickly toward me, my eagerness to find Don Diego's killer faded to dust.

I must have looked like quite the sight, a young girl—not quite a woman— in a colorful red and white dress riding a small mule in the middle of nowhere.

"Señorita, are you lost?" The rider asked me as he approached.

"No—" I hesitated, but found a courage I did not know I had. "I am looking for you."

"Me?" He laughed, but his eyes focused on me like a hawk. "Aren't you a little young to be chasing after men, chica?"

"I saw what you did last night—I know it was you who killed Don Diego."

He looked over his shoulder. The other men had not seemed to notice us.

"That pendejo got what he deserved. What business is it of yours?"

"They arrested my father. They think he is the one who killed him!"

The rider took off his sombrero and looked over at the rising sun. "What is your name, child?"

"I am María Herrera, and I am not afraid of you." Except I was, very afraid.

"Herrera ... I know that name."

"My family owned the large hacienda outside of San Miguel for many generations, until it was bought from us by Don Diego."

"Ah yes, I remember now. You come from a very proud family." His demeanor changed, and I now saw kindness in his eyes. "I am sorry about your father, María. My name is Pedro Martínez, and these are my cattle." He waved his sombrero toward the hundreds of longhorn cattle that were massed along the river. "I did not expect them to arrest another man for my crimes ... This is very troubling."

"You must return to town with me and tell them it was you who killed Don Diego, not my father. You must!"

"Yes, you are right ... but there are other things I must do first. I must take these cattle to Monterrey and sell them. Then I can use the money to—"

"I don't care about any of that, you must—"

"Here," he said as he tossed me a small round wooden canteen. "Why don't you give your mouth a rest for a moment."

I pulled the cork and took a couple of large gulps of the cool water, not realizing how thirsty I was. "Keep that," he said. "You will need it for your journey back."

He climbed down off of his horse and reached into his leather saddle bag. He pulled out a small tin box and motioned me over to a nearby cluster of rocks. "Get off that ... little mule of yours. It will do you good to stretch your legs." He sat down on a large flat stone and opened the box. He took out a roll of paper, a pen and a bottle of ink, and began writing.

When he was done, he carefully rolled the papers up and wrapped them with a piece of needlegrass. "I want you to take this letter to your father. I would ask you not to reveal my identity to anyone until he has had a chance to read it."

"A letter?"

"It's a proposal ... If he decides to accept it, things might work out better for both of us."

"A proposal? If you do not come with me, how will you even know what he decides?"

"If he refuses it, I will know when the federales come for me in Monterrey ... If he accepts, he will have to take me for my word that I will do what I say I will do."

I don't know why, but I trusted Señor Martínez.

When Chaparrita and I arrived back in town everyone stopped to stare at us. I must have looked like a bruja with my wild wind-swept hair and dust caked clothes. When we reached the jail, I slid gingerly off Chaparrita's back, rubbed her chin, and sent her home with a hard smack on the rump. The mule would be alright, I wasn't so sure about myself, or my father. It would all depend on Señor Martínez's mysterious proposal.

The jail was an old mud brick building built by the Spanish, with a large wooden door and enormous iron hinges. I had to push against the heavy door with all of my might just to crack it open enough to slip inside. The room was dark and sparse, except for a couple of guards who were standing around a long table in the back. A large fat one, with a face like a frog, noticed me and said, "Hey, what are you doing here? This is no place for children."

"I need to see my father, Señor Herrera."

They both started laughing. "The coward who killed Don Diego? No! You must leave."

I don't know why I said it, but I quickly blurted out, "Please. You don't understand. My mother is very sick, I think she might be dying."

They stopped laughing. "Isn't there someone else your family can send?"

"No, it's just me. Please, I don't know what to do … who will take care of me?"

I must have looked pretty pathetic with my wild hair and dirty dress. I even managed a few tears. The fat one shook his head and grabbed a large ring of keys off of the wall. "Follow me," he said impatiently.

I nodded and followed him through a series of doors into a dark stone passageway that smelled of sweat and hopelessness. We walked past several cells as my eyes searched the shadows for any sign of my father. Finally, he stopped in front of a large door with a tiny window near the top. I wasn't tall enough to reach it, so the guard placed a chair in front of the door for me to stand on.

"Five minutes," the guard said as he walked away.

I stood on the chair and looked through the window. My father was crouched in the corner of the small room, staring expressionlessly at the floor.

"Papa! Papa!" I whispered excitedly.

He raised his head and his eyes grew very large.

"My little flower, is that you?"

"Yes, Papa."

"What are you doing here, child, is everything alright? Where is your Mother?"

"I am sure she is fine, but that is not—I had to see you. I know that you are innocent. I saw the man who killed Don Pedro—I watched him do it."

"You do not need to make up stories for me, mija. Everything will be okay. They have no evidence against me—other than the drunken ravings of an old man."

"I am not making it up. His name is Pedro Martínez, and he gave me this letter—" I stuck the roll of papers through the tiny window.

My father reached out and took the papers, and then peered through the window at my filthy face. "What has happened to you? How did you come to possess this letter?"

"It doesn't matter, Papa. Please read it and tell me what it says."

My father held the paper up to the thin sliver of light that slipped through the small opening in the door. He read through the pages for several minutes in silence before folding them up and placing them in his pants pocket.

"Martínez admits that he did it ... he killed Don Diego."

"Let's show the letter to the guards," I said excitedly. "You can be free, Papa!"

"It's tempting ... but he also makes an interesting proposal." My father began to pace back and forth in the cell. This is always what he did when he was thinking. "Martínez says he had two brothers that were prospecting in the hills around San Miguel. He received a telegram from them two years ago that said they had found a rich vein of silver and were on there way to Monterrey to file their claim. That was the last he ever heard from them ..."

"What concern of that is ours?"

"He has been searching for his brothers ever since, trying to retrace their steps. He was able to track them as far as a small cantina in a village about thirty kilometers north of here. Several people there remembered his brothers, and said they had gotten drunk and boasted about the riches they had discovered to a man who worked in the cantina, a man named Diego Rivera. Martínez became convinced that this man had killed his brothers and stolen their claim." My father's eyes flared with anger, "That is how the pinche pendejo became rich—through his treachery." He spit on the floor. "Martínez came to town last night to confront Don Diego about his suspicions. He says that he had not intended to kill him, but that Don Diego had threatened to do to him what he had done to his brothers. In a rage, Martínez drew his knife and stabbed the cabron!"

My father had become quite animated, but he now stood quietly without speaking. Finally, he said, "But Martínez did not think that they would arrest another man for his crime ... He planned to sell his cattle in Monterrey and file a petition to revoke Don Diego's claim on his brothers' silver mine and seize his assets. He was sure that the telegram from his brothers, along with the witnesses he had found at the cantina, and the money he was willing to pay the politicians, would be enough for the judges to rule in his favor. But he now fears if the authorities know he killed Don Diego, it will destroy his case and they will have him arrested."

My eyes filled with tears, and I started to cry. "So, what does he want? For you to admit to a murder that you did not commit?"

"Please don't cry, my love … He only asks that we keep his secret long enough for him to obtain the deed to the silver mine and rights to Don Diego's estate. Then he will return to San Miguel and tell everyone the truth of what happened that night. He believes that once the court learns of Don Diego's treacheries, they will see his killing as a clear case of self-defense."

A light that I had not seen in many years returned to my father's eyes. "Martínez then promises to return our hacienda to me, to our family, as compensation for my sufferings—and our silence. That is why I must accept his proposal, to restore our family's fortunes—to restore our honor."

There was no trial, but the authorities kept my father in jail even though they had no evidence and no witnesses against him, only the drunken threats he had made toward Don Diego. It was agonizing to wake up every morning and keep my silence while my father languished in that horrible place. I could see the strain it was putting on him, and each time my mother and I visited, the dark rings under his eyes grew larger and his cheeks shallower. As the weeks passed, I began to question why I had trusted someone I did not know—a killer. But my father's faith in Señor Martínez never wavered. He saw salvation for himself, as well as our family, in Martínez's proposal and was prepared to stay in jail for as long as it took to reclaim our land.

Finally, after sixty-five long days of darkness Señor Martínez returned to San Miguel. He did not come alone. He brought with him a powerful lawyer named Sergio De La Vega, famous throughout Mexico for his powerful oratory, and even a federal judge to try his case. Some may have thought it was risky for him to return at all, but Pedro Martínez was now Don Pedro. The legal owner of a rich silver mine, and a man to be respected. Within a matter of hours my father was freed, and after a short trial the jury ruled that the killing of Don Diego had been justified.

True to his word, Don Pedro returned the hacienda to my father as payment for our hardships. With his name cleared and my family's legacy restored, my father is once again a proud and respected member of our community. He even stopped drinking. The rains returned in the spring, along with our fortunes, and soon we will have our first crops in many years. And me? Everyone calls me Doña María now, and in a few days I will celebrate my quinceañera. So many things have changed since the day of the fiesta, but I will never forget the night I witnessed the last dance of Don Diego.

THE GNOMES

A.M. Porter

When Frank Blanchard committed suicide by drowning himself in his backyard swimming pool, he tied two garden gnomes around his body to ensure he'd succeed. Afterwards, his wife, Mae, put them back on the lawn in front of a tub of white and pink petunias.

Mae's neighbours were suitably shocked, of course, even horrified. "What kind of person does that?" they asked, rhetorically, over dinner, or cocktails with friends on their backyard patios, or when they ran into each other at the Saturday farmers' market.

"Poor Edna," they might have added as an afterthought. Edna Purvis was the woman who lived right across the street from the Blanchards. Mid-fifties and never married, she had been good friends with Frank, and had only ever tolerated Mae. The presence of the gnomes could only sharpen her sense of loss—as well her dislike of Mae.

The first time Tamsin Bruce drove past the gnomes on her way to work, the sight of them naturally surprised her. Surprised and disturbed. As the pathologist's assistant at the County Coroner's office, she was the one who had given the items back to Mae once the Arden Police Department told her she might as well, since it was not a criminal case and there was no reason to keep them as evidence.

Three weeks had passed since the incident, a warm September giving way to a cool and rainy October. Two weeks since Frank had been eulogized and buried, with a big turnout at the funeral, coverage in the local papers, and an obituary in the *Globe and Mail*. The third morning Tamsin drove past the gnomes, grinning diabolically from their patch of lawn, she decided to say something to her boss, Jack Treadaway.

"Don't you find it incredibly weird and suspicious?" she asked.

Dr. Treadaway just pursed his lips and shook his head slowly. "Weird, yes. Suspicious, no," he replied. "A case of suicide. Open and shut." The man tended to speak like that, in clipped phrases, like a kind of verbal shorthand. "Left a suicide note. Remember?"

He had, and she did. There was really no doubt at all that Frank had written and signed it, Dr. Treadaway immediately recognizing the handwriting and signature. He had recently purchased a copy Frank's latest novel for his wife's birthday, and Frank had written a dedication on the flyleaf.

"I'm sorry it has to be this way," the suicide note had said, "but everything must come to an end at some point, and I feel I have no other choice."

What's more, the autopsy showed no evidence of a blow to the head, no marks, bruises, or contusions anywhere on the body. The tox screen had come back negative. The lab analysis of stomach contents didn't indicate the presence of alcohol. And they found no prints, of course, on the statuary. Just two lengths of wet rope, knotted around their necks and wrapping the body.

According to Mae, her husband was often depressed. What with him being a writer, and not just any writer but one whose work garnered both critical acclaim— 'shattering,' 'exquisitely written,' 'deeply introspective'—and poor sales, this only made sense to Dr. Treadaway.

Yet, Tamsin recalled, there had been nothing in his medical records suggesting Frank suffered from depression. She knew, because she'd checked. He apparently hadn't talked to his doctor about it, or been prescribed anti-depressants. So, aside from Dr. Treadaway's prejudices, it was really only Mae's word. Now the fact that she'd put those horrible gnomes back on her lawn instead of throwing them out made Tamsin wish that they had looked into Frank Blanchard's death a little more carefully.

It struck her that the gnomes must symbolize something for the not-so-grieving widow: Triumph? Her ability to outsmart everyone? But as just a pathology assistant, certified for less than two years, Tamsin knew her opinions on the matter didn't carry a whole lot of weight. Dr. Treadaway had held his position as coroner for over three decades; the police trusted him and his conclusions. It may have been an odd way to take one's life, but some people were just like that. Odd.

Later that morning, she searched the Internet for Frank's bio and book reviews and read it four times. All the praise from literary critics and academics seemed so distant from the reality of Frank's life, so unreal compared to the ordinariness of it. Maybe he had decided his was a life no longer worth living.

Over lunch break, Tamsin dug out the report she'd filled out three weeks earlier. It was pretty thin. The file still contained the suicide note and, yes, it looked perfectly legit. It took up the upper third of a whole sheet of pale grey letter paper, and was written in a sure and tidy hand. It didn't look as though it had been trimmed or torn from a larger sheet of paper, like she'd once seen on an episode of *Morse* on television.

Sighing, she put the page back into its manila folder and bit into her sandwich. She started thinking about all the reasons someone like Mae might want to do away with a husband like Frank. A big life insurance policy? Frank's had been nothing special, with a modest payout of just $90,000. A lover? That notion almost made her choke on her sandwich. Mae Blanchard was neither attractive nor young, the last woman she could ever imagine arousing another man's passion. Indeed, Tamsin had always found it nothing short of miraculous that she'd even managed to get a husband, let alone a famous writer, like Frank—although he wasn't published back then, was just a guy with a low-level job at the Arden Utilities Commission. While not exactly handsome, he'd always seemed kind and polite. Modest, despite the accolades, even rather shy. He had been fully clothed when he threw himself into the pool—blue button-down shirt, beige slacks, socks and lace-up shoes on his feet—as if he didn't want anyone to see his naked body. Only Dr. Treadaway. And me, of course, Tamsin thought.

She hadn't known Frank well, although she'd first met Mae back in high school. She had come in one day when Tamsin was in Grade 11, substituting for the history teacher, who was off sick. Schoolmarmish and unfashionably dressed—even for a small town like Arden—she looked as though it would kill her to smile. The teacher, Mr. Kenny, had placed everyone in seats in alphabetical order and Tamsin had been stuck right in front of his desk, which she hated. So, when Miss Eckert, as she was then, showed up, it seemed like an opportunity to move back into a different seat. The girl's basketball team was playing an away game that afternoon, and the seat she chose belonged to a girl called Yundt, Myrna Yundt.

Mae did the roll call, Tamsin raised her hand when Myrna's name was called, and there was a sudden silence. Mae looked her over, lips pursed, and said, sarcastically, "Well I don't know who you are, but you are certainly not Myrna Yundt." All the students burst out laughing. Mae had, it turned out, taught Myrna in elementary school. Unaware of that, Tamsin had felt like an idiot, and the following forty minutes of class, total torture. It was a small thing, a silly thing, yet even now, all these years later, she could still remember the embarrassment, could feel herself blushing all over again. Upset, she scrunched the remains of her sandwich into a wax-paper ball and threw it into the waste bin.

Maybe, she thought, she was making another mistake, letting an age-old resentment nurture baseless suspicions and cloud her judgement. Maybe Dr. Treadaway was right. A case of suicide. Open and shut.

For the rest of the day, Tamsin tried to focus on her work. There was plenty to do; paperwork to fill out from a fatal car accident, notes to input in the computer, and supplies to order. She pushed the entire matter out of her mind until five o'clock, when, walking through the parking lot to her car, she ran into Pete Cameron, Arden's chief of police—and a cousin of Tamsin's ex-boyfriend, Jamie.

Pete struck a lot of people in Arden as rather young to be police chief, even though he was in his 40s. Part of that had to do with his affable, easy-going manner. A real salt-of-the-earth type, he spoke leisurely, calmly, as if nothing could truly perturb him. "Hey there, Tammy," he said, casually placing his hands on his hips. "How's it going?"

"Great," she said, not meaning it. She hated it when he called her 'Tammy.' "Looking forward to raking the leaves this weekend, cleaning out the fishpond, and digging out my puffy winter jacket."

"Oh, come on," Pete laughed. "Getting a bit ahead of yourself, aren't you?"

"There's nothing wrong with being prepared," Tamsin objected. Jamie used to bug her about her fanatic tidiness, about the way she double-checked the locks, chided people in the park for letting their dogs run off-leash, and stowed bottled water, extra batteries, and small denomination bills in the basement in case of a really bad winter storm. The kind of guy who removed the rubber snow mats from his car in July, he'd accused her of being an obsessive compulsive. But that's just the way she was; it was what made her good at her job.

Pete laughed again, and she rolled her eyes. And then, before she could stop herself, egged on probably by the depressing weather and her depressing thoughts about Mae Blanchard, she went ahead and blurted it out. The question she was still dying to ask.

"Have you noticed that Frank Blanchard's wife has put those gnomes her husband used to drown himself back out onto her lawn?"

Pete gave her a penetrating look, then shrugged. "Yeah, I saw that the other day," he said slowly. "Kind of unnerving, aren't they? I don't know what people see in them myself."

"Well, that wasn't really my point, Pete. When you looked into it, were there any—?"

"I know," he interrupted her. "I know what your point is, Tam." She kept glaring, saying nothing, until he finally added, "Look, I did ask a few people about Frank's state of mind at the time. His wife said he was depressed. His agent said he was moody, not his usual self. And his editor said he'd become fed up with the agent and was hoping to find a new one. So it seemed it could go either way, but the fact is, and you know this, your PM showed no indication that there was any other hand in this but Frank's. Mae wasn't even there."

With that, Pete turned towards the office, saying, "See you around," and Tamsin got into her car, still annoyed. With him, herself, or Mae, she couldn't say.

The sky, as she drove home, was the colour of a tin can, mottled with clouds. The trees along the familiar streets she took were starting to assume the harlequin colours of fall, deep and dense in the waning light. She drove by the Blanchard house, its nothing-special, white-brick façade a bald backdrop to a leaf-covered lawn, Mae's fussy flowerbeds, and those damn gnomes.

Back home, Tamsin made herself a vodka tonic and, still wearing her jacket, sat outside to drink it. Leaves were falling in her backyard too, tumbling in the breeze to colour the grass with a carpet of gold, and roofing the surface of her koi pond. She walked over to check on the fish, Sputnik, Basil and Bunny. Tamsin had given them names, not daring to tell Jamie, who would only have jeered. Clearing away some of the leaves, she was suddenly disheartened by how the year seemed to have gone by so quickly, and she thought about Frank again. Had he too been disappointed with life, with his books and the modest living they had afforded him over the years?

On her way to work the next day, she stopped at the Blanchard house instead of continuing on to the coroner's office. Mustering courage, she rang the doorbell and, as Mae opened it, wondered for the hundredth time what Frank had ever seen in her.

So plain and unprepossessing with that dumpy body. The awful haircut that looked like a cheap wig.

She looked at Tamsin blankly, cold and unsmiling, and she couldn't help but wonder if Mae recognized her from high school, remembered what a fool she'd been, pretending to be someone else just so she could move seats for one 45-minute history class.

But if she did, Tamsin couldn't tell. She pulled out her ID and said she'd like to take another look at the pool in her back yard.

Mae's eyebrows pricked up just for a second but otherwise her deadened facial expression didn't change. She didn't say anything either, just stood aside and held out her hand in a little flourish, like a maître d' showing a diner to a restaurant table.

'Bitch,' Tamsin thought. "Thanks," she said, walking into the house and through a beige living room, where sliding glass doors gave out onto a patio dotted with cheap plastic chairs. About twenty feet further, down a gentle slope, was the swimming pool.

She stood there and looked at it for several minutes, as if waiting for it to somehow disclose its secrets. As if the flat surface and turquoise painted concrete beneath it could impart some kind of clue that would explain everything.

"What is it you're looking for anyway?" Mae asked irritably.

Tamsin walked around the pool, looking at the condition of the cement surround, the steps heading down into shallow end at the back, the leaves floating on the water. She leaned over and checked the water filter. There was nothing.

"Just tying up loose ends," she replied.

"What loose ends?"

Tamsin didn't bother to answer. Emerging again, the front door shut unceremoniously behind her, she noticed Edna Purvis in her front yard, raking leaves. Bundled up in a stylish wool coat and patterned scarf, she worked energetically, gathering the leaves into a large pile, ready for the tall paper bag standing like a sentinel beside it. Tamsin thought about crossing the street to talk to her, hesitated, feeling unsure of herself, then went ahead. It was not like she had anything to lose.

Edna looked surprised as Tamsin walked up the flagstone path. "Sorry to bother you," she said. "But I was wondering if I could maybe talk to you for a minute? About, um, Frank?"

Leaning on the rake, catching her breath, Edna almost frightened her with the piercing gaze of her blue eyes. "Maybe you'd better come in," she said finally.

The rest of the day would have been a write-off, workwise, if Dr. Treadaway, far from pleased at her late arrival, hadn't found so much to keep Tamsin busy. She was dying to tell him about her conversation with Edna Purvis, about how she'd admitted that things had become serious between her and Frank, how he had told her he wanted to divorce his wife, and how badly he wanted "a fresh start. I didn't say anything to Pete Cameron about it," she'd said. "I didn't want it to get around and besides, there didn't seem to be any point anymore." It meant that Frank maybe wasn't all that depressed. It might even have meant that Mae was enraged by his wanting to leave her, except that Edna had no idea if Frank had said anything to her or not. It still wasn't enough, Tamsin felt, to make her interrupt a man who was already in a bad mood that day.

The next morning, she called Frank's publisher in Toronto and was put through to his editor, a woman named Karen Hanover. She didn't sound all that surprised to hear from her, Tamsin noticed. She asked a few questions about Frank, and Karen told her that he had always struck her as the sort of man who cared only about one thing, and that was his writing. "But lately," she added, "he'd started thinking about sales. It really started to matter to him, to bother him. He wondered why his books never seemed to get translated and sold in other markets. I told him the English-language market was already quite a substantial one, and that it wasn't all that uncommon that worthy books didn't bring in big sales, but it didn't seem to appease him. He said he wanted to find a new agent, someone who would be more proactive, as he put it. It's funny, but it was a word I could never have imagined Frank even using before that."

Tamsin dug out the Blanchard file again, and looked at that note he'd left. All at once it dawned on her that it could have been the final page of a letter, a letter to his agent, simply telling him that he was moving on to another, more supportive one. She felt a cold chill run down her back, convinced suddenly that Mae had to have set the whole thing up. But how?

Over the next few hours, she found herself so distracted, she could hardly work. She had to do things over and over again because she kept losing her train of thought halfway through each task. It was as if her brain were on trial, being asked that very same question—how?—with each answer quickly disproven. Every fifteen minutes or so, she picked up the phone, ready to call Pete Cameron, before putting it down again, overwhelmed by doubts and indecision.

By the time she left the office to drive home, it was already getting dark. She was so rattled she took a different, more circuitous route home, just so she wouldn't have to drive past the Blanchard house and see those dreadful little figures that had held a man down while he drowned.

She knew she should eat something; she hadn't been able to face food since breakfast, but instead she made herself another vodka tonic. A stiff one. Shivering, she walked through the house, switching on lamps and the television set, telling herself to get a grip for heaven's sake. She'd call Pete Cameron in the morning and that would be the end of it.

Returning to the kitchen, she flipped the switch for the backyard lights as well. The cherry tree, the few clumps of dead flowers, and the fishpond were immediately illuminated, soft blurry pools of yellow glowing among the shrubbery.

Then she noticed that the back porch was still in darkness, even though she knew she'd recently replaced the old light bulb in the exterior fitting. Sighing, she put down her drink, got the kitchen ladder, and went outside to fiddle with it. The bulb was still there, but loose; a quick turn of the wrist had it shining again.

About to go back inside, something in the yard caught the corner of her eye. Something at the koi pond, which had no reason to be there, and she felt her heart jump. A pair of gnomes, just like Mae's, just like the ones that had been tied around Frank, standing on either side of the pond. They seemed to be defying her, with their grotesque faces, their frozen smiles, like other-worldly, evil trolls. Only Mae could have put them there, Tamsin was sure, placing them in her backyard as an open act of confrontation. Perfect, she thought: more proof to tell Pete about.

She strode out angrily from the porch towards the fishpond, ready to grab the gnomes and tempted to smash them to pieces on the patio. Suddenly she felt a sharp pain against the upper part of her foot, one first and then the other, a stinging blow that tripped her and sent her plunging forward. She hit the water face down and felt rope against her neck, then something heavy pulled in over her back. As she flailed and tried to right herself, another weight fell onto her legs. The cold water had hit her like an electric shock and she kept on struggling, still trying to pull herself free. But she couldn't even feel the bottom of the pond, only the horrible sensation of something large and scaly scrape across her face.

Twisting and turning in the tangle of ropes, she almost thought she could see something looming over the surface of the pond, as at last she understood how. How Mae Blanchard had done it. But by then, her limbs were growing numb and her lungs, desperate for air, exploding in pain.

All at once an upward force, like a film on rewind, seemed to pull her back again, out of the water, and drop her hard onto the ground. Coughing and heaving, she gasped for air. A hand was slapping her on the back, and rolling over, she saw him.

"You okay?"

"Jamie," she spluttered. "Oh my God! What are you doing here?"

He drew himself erect and looked at her, frowning in confusion, as if surprised at the question.

"I, erm, I think I left the mitre bit for my drill here. I came back to get it."

"God," she said, climbing unsteadily to her feet. "That was last year!"

"I know. Are you okay?" he asked again.

They went inside to the warmth of the house and Jamie told her how he had been parked on the street in front of the house, waiting for her to get back, when he got a call on his cell phone. By the time he hung up and rang the doorbell, there was no answer, even though he'd seen all the lights come on. "So I just went around back and saw you charging into the pond."

He cast a glance outside at the pond and saw the wire, a horizontal metallic gleam that stretched tight from one side of the pond to the other, attached to a pair of tent pegs. "That explains it," he said.

"She snuck in and set it up, the same way she did for Frank," Tamsin said, quietly.

"I know. I know. While I was on the phone, I saw her run out along the side of the house and jump into her car just as you arrived. So weird."

"You saw her?" Tamsin grabbed his upper arm excitedly. "You saw Mae Blanchard?"

"No." he shook his head. "I saw Edna Purvis."

"Yeah, you kinda got it right," said Pete Cameron, "but you also got it mostly wrong."

Tamsin had come in to make a statement, but Pete had already talked to Edna and arrested her for first degree murder and attempted murder. "That might get reduced to assault," he remarked.

Edna hadn't held out for long under questioning. She had wept profusely, embarrassed more than anything else, it had seemed to Pete. She admitted that Frank had come over with his carefully written letter to his agent, wanting her opinion, hoping it didn't sound callous. Edna had suggested he make a clean break with everything, with his staid lifestyle and his unhappy marriage, not just his agent; start all over again and move in with her. But Frank had been shocked, she'd conceded, aghast at the idea of divorcing Mae. Edna couldn't believe it. After waiting so long for him, she said, she'd let the anger and bitterness get the better of her.

Setting him up for a fall the night Mae always went out to visit her mother at Greenwood Court Retirement Home had been easy. Finding the letter on his desk and stealing the page, a piece of cake, while Mae's inexplicable attachment to her gnomes and Tamsin's suspicions had created an even more optimal outcome, an unexpected bonus. Frank dead and his wife incriminated for that death.

It wasn't the conclusion Tamsin had expected or wanted. It didn't fit with her image of either woman. Wiping the ballpoint pen Pete had given her to sign her statement, she stared at the pages lying in front of her. But in her mind, she was seeing confusion rather than order. Bewilderment instead of any sort of proper resolution. People in Arden were talking about her now, she knew, with admiration and even a certain thrill. As if she were some kind of latter-day Miss Marple. No one knew how she really felt.

With the exception, perhaps, of Mae Blanchard. She could imagine her face, smug and cold, smiling grimly like a gnome.

CHARLIE'S WAR

John M. Floyd

A light snow was falling as Charlie Reardon left the diner and made his way down Madison Street. He stopped at a sidewalk bench at the corner of Madison and Belmont and sat down, his elbows on his knees and his eyes on the building across the street.

Two minutes later an old blue Ford pulled up to the curb twenty feet away and cut its engine. A tall redhaired man in a watchcap and overcoat climbed out of the car, cupped his hands to light a cigarette, and strolled over to the bench. Charlie glanced at him, then went back to staring at the now-darkened windows across the road. It was almost six o'clock. Streetlights were flickering to life, halos of yellow in the mist.

"Rosie sent me to look for you," said the tall man. "Where's your cell phone?"

"Battery died."

"I figured. Also figured I might find you here."

Without turning, Charlie said, "You a mind reader now, Morgan?"

"Only if it's a weak mind. Yours is easy. It's snowing, by the way."

Charlie smiled, and pictured his brother-in-law smiling too, around the cigarette. And turned to follow his gaze.

"That's where it all started," Morgan said, solemn again. "Ten years ago today. Right?"

"Wrong. That's where it ended. If you remember, it started five miles north."

They turned together, to face each other. The snow was coming down harder now.

"I remember," Morgan said.

Charlie sighed. What Morgan didn't remember, because Charlie had never told him, was that what happened all those years ago in that building across the street almost didn't happen at all. When Charlie Reardon walked here from the other side of town that day, it wasn't because it was *his* idea. It was someone else's. It seemed to make sense, at the time.

This was a place of memories, yes. Good *and* bad. But it was also a mystery.

Ten years earlier
11:50 a.m., November 19, 2009

Charlie sat on a carpet of fallen leaves at the edge of a city park in the 1800 block of North Madison, half a mile from his childhood home. He was leaning against the trunk of an elm tree and watching the front entrance of the shop next door. Beidelman's Fine Jewelry. What he didn't know was that someone was watching *him*. If Charlie had been more careful about watching the store he wouldn't have attracted attention, and if he'd been smart enough to know he was being observed, he'd have stopped watching the store. But, although Charlie Reardon had been accused of a lot of things in his twenty-three years, he'd never been accused of being careful. Or smart.

As a result, he looked up from his study of the comings and goings of Mr. Beidelman's customers and pushed back the bill of his baseball cap to see a uniformed policeman standing over him, thumbs hooked in his gunbelt like an Old West sheriff.

"What's your name, son?" the cop asked. Though there probably wasn't a dozen years' difference in their ages.

"Joe Smith," Charlie said.

"And what are you doing?"

"I'm sitting under a tree."

The cop—his nameplate said COLLIER—cocked his head like a puppy Charlie had once owned, as a boy. But he didn't recall the puppy narrowing its eyes and scowling.

"You been sittin' there almost an hour, Mr. Smith."

"Want me to move, so you can rake these leaves?"

Patiently, Officer Collier said, "I want you to answer me a question: You thinking about buying a ring for your girlfriend, maybe? A necklace for your mother?"

"What are you talking about?"

Collier shrugged. "Just wondering. Seems you been looking at that jewelry store there, all this time."

Charlie squinted at the building. "That's a jewelry store?"

"That's what the sign says."

"I didn't notice."

Behind him, somewhere nearby, a dog yapped, a see-saw creaked, a baby cried. It was a nice day, warm for November, and the park was crowded. An older kid shouted something and another answered. Charlie wondered why they weren't in school.

"Is that yours?" Collier was pointing to a battered duffel bag on the grass between them.

"Whose else would it be?"

The cop looked around. "And is that your car?" He nodded toward an ancient and dented Chevy parked some distance away. Charlie had never seen it before, but could understand why someone might think it was his. It looked just like his duffel bag. Old and tired.

"I don't have a car," he said.

Deeper in the park, music was blaring from what sounded like an ancient PA system. Officer Collier turned again to the jewelry store, studied it a minute, and fixed Charlie with another stare. Elvis was singing "Suspicious Minds." Appropriate, Charlie thought.

"I plan to remember you, Joe Smith. You understand what I'm saying?"

"Yes, I believe I do."

"Good." The cop hitched his belt a little higher, adjusted his hat, and marched away.

When he was out of sight, Charlie blew out a breath and wiped his sweaty palms on the legs of his jeans. He'd attracted the attention of the Law plenty of times—MPs, mostly—but rarely *before* he'd done anything wrong. He wondered if he should rethink his latest plans.

Those plans hadn't required a lot of thought to begin with. Charlie Reardon's current station in life was easily summarized: homeless and hopeless. Both of those adjectives were fairly recent—when he'd returned from Iraq six months ago he at least had some savings and a few prospects. They hadn't lasted long. None of the three jobs he tried had worked out. More accurately, *he* hadn't worked out. Post-traumatic stress disorder had been around for a long time, but most employers didn't seem to know much or care much about it. The only thing Charlie's bosses cared about was that all those headaches and dizzy spells and stomach problems he'd brought back with him from the desert war were damaging his job performance. Now, two weeks after his latest firing, here he sat, owing a stack of bills and owning nothing but some clothes and a duffel bag, and seriously considering a jewelry-store heist as his best and only career path. On second thought, he found himself wondering why he felt he could do a better job at that than he'd done with all the other things he'd attempted in his relatively short life.

The truth was, the only thing Charlie had ever been good at was baseball—and even that hadn't lasted long. All those pitching records he set in high school meant nothing after he ruined his knee sliding into home during his first college game. The full scholarship his right arm earned him vanished in a blur of surgeries and medication, and even though he was sadly informed that he would never play organized sports again he was declared healthy enough for Uncle Sam's Army, which at that time—his mother was deceased and his father long gone—seemed his only option. As it turned out, Private Reardon was no better at the military than at anything else, but at least he survived his expense-paid tour of the Middle East. And now here he was. Honorably discharged and dishonorably dysfunctional.

Suddenly he was aware of yet another person watching him. Thirty feet away, a small black woman with a patch over one eye sat at a picnic table in the shade of a giant oak that seemed to be unaware of the time of year. The other trees were almost bare of leaves; this one blazed ten different shades of red and orange in the noonday sun. As Charlie was about to turn away from her gaze, he saw the woman raise one hand and beckon to him.

What now?

She waved again, more insistent this time. Finally Charlie rose to his feet, picked up his duffel, and walked uncertainly to the picnic table. The woman was perched on its wooden top, her sneakered feet resting on the seat. She brushed leaves from the tabletop beside her, and he sat down. Elvis was now crooning "Blue Hawaii," which was where Charlie wished he was.

"Are you a cop, too?" he asked the woman.

"I'm a friend." And something in her kind, wrinkled face confirmed that. Whatever it was that this woman wanted, she meant him no harm. "You're Charles Reardon," she added.

It wasn't a question. Somehow, in spite of being twenty pounds heavier and sporting a Grizzly Adams beard, he'd been recognized by someone. How was that possible?

When he made no reply, she smiled. The eyepatch and its strap around her head reminded him of Captain Kidd, and should've made her appear sinister, or at least unsettling. It didn't.

"I know things, young man," she said, in a soft voice. "I can see more with one eye than most people can with two."

And what was *that* supposed to mean?

"Besides"—she tilted her head almost the way the policeman had done ten minutes ago—"I remember you. You were quite a star, a few years ago. A 110-mile-per-hour fastball, the papers said. You threw so hard your catchers wore extra padding in their mitts."

"Don't believe everything you read," Charlie said. "Tell me again—who *are* you?"

She seemed to consider that. "I'm someone who knows you've had a hard life. And who knows you brought part of that war home with you."

"And ..."

"And I can make it better."

Charlie frowned. "What?"

"It's not just money you need, Charles Reardon. You need confidence, and purpose. You need to regain a feeling of self-worth."

He couldn't help smiling. Of all the things this woman reminded him of, a psychiatrist wasn't one of them. "You're saying you can help me with that?"

"Yes."

"How?"

"I have something to give you. Something that will redirect your path."

"My path?"

"You'll see," she said, and reached into a cloth purse the size of a potato sack.

What she took from the purse struck Charlie speechless. He couldn't have been more stunned if she'd pulled out a car battery, or a machine gun, or a white rabbit.

In her hand was a baseball, its stitched cover scarred with use. A baseball with his autograph written on it. He remembered it; he pitched that ball all nine innings of the game that won the state championship his senior year in high school.

"Where did you—"

"From the display case in the public library," she said. "It's been there six years."

"You ... stole it?"

"Not exactly. They were, how should I say?—rearranging things."

It took Charlie a moment to catch on.

"They were getting rid of it," he said.

She shrugged her bony shoulders. "Restructuring the lobby, they called it. In any event, it's yours now. Use it well."

"What do you mean?"

"As I said, you'll see."

I know what I'll see, he thought, tucking the ball into the pocket of his jacket. *I'll see if I can sell it.* But he doubted it. Old athletes fade away faster than old soldiers. "What I'm wondering is, how'd you find me? How'd you know I was here today?"

She shook her head. "That's not important. What's important is that you shouldn't do what you've been planning to do."

That shook him a bit, too. She knew about the jewelry store?

"Let me qualify that," she added. "You shouldn't do it *here*."

"What do you mean, here?"

The old woman leaned closer. "I know your history, my boy. Your troubles. I know you need the money, and I care not a whit for old man Beidelman over there, and his diamond necklaces. But you need to do this *right*."

Charlie could think of no reply to that.

"You know about Reuben Miller? You know who he is?"

He frowned. "I know he's held up six banks around here in the past few months."

"And killed six people. One at the scene of each robbery. Way I heard it, none of them opposed him or tried to catch him or hurt him—he killed 'em for no reason, except to scare off those who might oppose him later. To set an example. You get my meaning?"

"No. What does all that have to do with me?"

"It can help you, that's what." She lowered her voice, her single eye boring into him. "I told you I know you, Charles Reardon. And I do. I know you don't want to hurt anybody. I know you don't even own a gun. Correct?"

"Are you kidding? I wouldn't be able to afford a bullet."

"Well, my point is, if you're thinking of a robbery—"

"Wait a minute. I didn't say that."

"Okay. If you *were* thinking of a robbery …" She paused. "You want to hear the rest?"

He shrugged. "Why not?"

"If you were thinking of that, and you don't want to hurt anyone, you should go to a bank and hand one of the tellers a note saying you're Reuben Miller and you want her to fill that duffel bag there with hundred-dollar bills. She'll do it and do it quick because so far nobody knows exactly what Miller looks like—he leaves his name but he's always worn a mask—and she'll be scared of getting killed like all the others he's killed. You won't need a gun, and you won't have to worry about cameras or getting recognized because of your cap and that godawful beard on your face. Or about trying to convert stolen jewelry to cash. You follow me so far?"

Charlie swallowed and nodded. He couldn't quite believe what he was hearing. *This* was supposed to help him regain a feeling of self-worth?

But something made him keep quiet. Even the park had fallen silent. The music had stopped.

"When it's done," she said, "you walk out of the bank and down an alley to a café

I'll tell you about and go into their bathroom and lock the door and shave that beard off. Maybe trim your hair back off your ears. Then stuff the money into your pockets, ditch your cap and bag, and walk out and disappear. Nobody escapes from a robbery on foot—they'll be looking for a getaway car while you stroll off into the sunset."

"Sunset?"

"That's right. You need to do it this afternoon, a Thursday just before quitting time. But it has to be at a bank that Reuben Miller would choose—large enough to be worth his time and small enough not to have a security force."

"So what are you saying?"

"I'm saying the ideal place is on the south side of town, five miles straight down this street and one block west. First Citizens Bank. Don't take a bus or a cab, you need to walk there so nobody'll remember you, and stop on the way to pick up things for your bag that you'll need later—scissors, shaving cream, razor, sunglasses." She dug into her purse again and came out with a bill. "Twenty dollars should cover it."

Charlie sat there a moment, looking at the twenty. Finally he met her gaze. "I can't figure this. Why are you helping me this way? Why do you *care*?"

"I told you already—I can see things, things you can't. Okay?" She pressed the cash into his palm and stared into his eyes. "One day you'll understand."

Somehow he doubted he would. This was too crazy. But he agreed with her on one thing. Those thoughts were for later. For the first time in awhile, he'd been given a plan.

Ten minutes later, after hearing the rest of what he thought of as a mission briefing—he was reminded of Jim Phelps and two smoking spools of audio tape—Charlie picked up his bag, pocketed the twenty, and headed south. He knew where to go and what to do when he got there.

If that wasn't a plan, what was?

Charlie drew a long breath and let it out. Four hours and five miles since his meeting with his eyepatched and fortune-telling friend, he was now sitting on a wooden bench on the corner of Madison and Belmont, across the street from First Citizens Bank. He had no watch, but the clock on the side of the building told him it was almost 4:30. It even gave him the temperature, in big red numbers. Fifty-two degrees. Cool but not cold—perfect for the bulky jacket that would later hide his unauthorized withdrawal of funds. He took a last look around, tucked his gym bag under his arm, pulled his cap low over his eyes, and crossed the street.

The bank lobby was, as the old woman predicted, only moderately crowded.

A middle-of-the-month Thursday afternoon. Three teller stations lined the wall, with only a couple of customers queued up at each. Trying not to be noticeable, Charlie strolled to the line farthest from the front door and took his place behind a baldheaded man in a gray suit. No one paid him any attention. With sweaty fingers Charlie checked his shirt pocket. The holdup message was there, printed on a folded slip of lined notepaper.

The place was too loud, he thought. Too much stone, too much tile. Voices rang, footsteps echoed. He tried to look relaxed, but couldn't help glancing around. He saw a short young woman with reddish hair enter from the street, pushing an elderly lady in a wheelchair. Two middle-aged men in dark suits were studying a document, passing the pages across a table to each other and checking things off a list. A woman in a glass-walled office tapped the keys of a computer on her desktop.

The customer at the head of Charlie's line finished her transaction and left, and the bald guy in front of him stepped forward. Charlie followed. It wouldn't be long now. He took the note from his pocket and cupped it in his palm, ready to show it to the teller when it was his turn. He could feel his heart beating, could feel his damp shirt sticking to his back.

And then he heard the last thing he wanted or expected to hear:

A scream.

A blonde woman in one of the other lines had turned and was shrieking to high heaven, one hand on her chest and the other pointing toward the front entrance.

"Shut up!" a man's distorted voice said, and the woman clapped both hands over her mouth. The whole lobby fell silent. Charlie saw, when he turned to look, the reason for the scream, and the muffled reply. The speaker had tied a black cloth over his nose and mouth.

He stood just inside the front doors, a tall, heavy man in a dark coat and gloves, and held a silver-plated revolver with a barrel almost a foot long. He moved it in a slow arc, covering everybody in the room. "My name's Reuben Miller," he said. "Look at me. All of you."

Almost everyone did. The young woman pushing the wheelchair was closest to the masked man, and with trembling hands she swiveled the chair so that both she and its occupant were facing him. But the elderly lady sat with her head bowed and staring at her lap.

"I said look at me!" he shouted to her.

"She can't," the younger woman said. "She can't raise her head."

Reuben Miller's ice-cold gaze shifted to her. "In that case," he said, "she can be my example for today." And raised his pistol.

"Wait!" The young woman stepped between him and the wheelchair. "Please. She's my mother."

"That's too bad, for you both." Miller cocked the revolver and took aim.

Later, Charlie Reardon would remember wishing he'd brought a gun after all. He hadn't—but he'd brought something else. Moments earlier, when the daughter moved to shield her mother, that didn't just put her between the gunman and the wheelchair; it put her between the gunman and Charlie. Which could've been unfortunate, but she was short and Miller was tall and the distance between Charlie and Miller was about thirty feet. Half the distance from the pitcher's mound to home plate.

In one smooth motion Charlie took the baseball from his pocket, swiveled right, planted his feet, cocked his right arm, and snapped it forward as hard as he could, as hard as he'd ever thrown a ball in his life. Half a second later, as Reuben Miller's finger was tightening on the trigger of his revolver, a rock-hard missile slammed into the center of his forehead at more than a hundred miles an hour. Miller's head whipped back, his body went limp as a ragdoll, and his eyeballs rolled upward as if to check on the giant dent that had suddenly appeared in his skull. Just before he crashed to the floor, his pistol fell also, discharged, and blew a hole through the baseboard of the east wall.

It was the only shot fired that day. The masked robber and murderer Reuben Miller lay face-up and motionless on the white tiles, arms and legs pointing in four different directions.

For a long moment, a dozen employees and customers stood frozen, their ears ringing from the gunshot. When they woke from their daze, two of those people—the daughter and her wheelchair-bound mother—clutched each other and sobbed.

Everyone else turned to look at Charlie Reardon.

Less than five minutes later Charlie and three bankers—the manager and two VPs— sat together at a walnut conference table. No one seemed to know what to say. On the faces of the two men and one woman was an odd mixture of wonder, relief, gratitude, and reverence. As for Charlie, he figured he probably looked more surprised than anything. Not only because of what had happened but because of what hadn't. He had been elevated, in the space of several seconds, from about-to-be criminal to the Savior of the Day. Outside the tall oak door of the boardroom, the lobby was a booming chorus of voices.

When at last the door opened, the man who entered the room was not the bank president, or the sheriff, or the chief of police. It was the cop Charlie Reardon had met this morning at the park on North Madison Street. Officer Collier. He didn't look as shocked to see Charlie as Charlie was to see him.

Collier glanced at each of the bankers in turn and said, "Can you give us a minute?"

Silently the three employees filed out, and he closed the door and locked it.

"Mr. Smith," he said. "We meet again."

Charlie could think of no good response. Lamely he said, "Aren't you on the wrong side of town, Officer?"

"I might ask you the same thing."

"I had some business here."

"Under the name Joe Smith?" Collier asked. "Or Charles Reardon?"

Charlie blinked. "Where'd you hear that name?"

"I didn't hear it. I saw it. It's written on an old baseball I found out there in the lobby." Collier took a seat facing Charlie across the table and took off his hat. "Like most folks around here, I remember your name, Charlie. I just didn't recognize you earlier, with that black thicket on your face." He paused and added, "Don't look so sad. After tonight's newscasts and tomorrow morning's papers, your name'll be more recognizable than the governor's."

Charlie shook his head. "Not because I want it to be." A sudden thought hit him. "Was that really Reuben Miller?"

"He said he was, or so I'm told. And so far, he's always worked alone."

Charlie swallowed. "Is he dead?"

"Not literally. He's breathing. He's on his way to the hospital. But I'm not sure if he'll ever wake up, and it'll be no loss if he doesn't. At the very least, you bashed his brains in."

"Good," Charlie said.

The room went silent. Outside, the lobby had grown even noisier.

"Just for the record," Collier said, "why were you carrying a baseball in your pocket?"

Charlie shrugged. "It was on display, in an exhibit. They were gonna throw it away."

"Good thing they didn't."

Another silence passed. Charlie said, "Are we done here? I'd like to get—"

"Just one question." Collier hesitated, then asked, "Why'd you do it?"

Charlie was asking himself the same thing. "I don't know. I guess I didn't think. I was just standing there, and when I saw what was about to happen ..."

Collier leaned forward in his seat. "I'll tell you what *did* happen. According to a passel of witnesses, you stopped a robbery and saved at least two lives. Maybe more."

That triggered another thought. "If all that's true—why are you in here talking to me?"

The cop sat back again and fixed him with a stare. "Because of this," he said, and held up a folded piece of lined notebook paper.

Charlie felt his stomach turn over.

"I picked it up off the floor. One of the other customers said he saw you drop it, during all the excitement."

Charlie just sat there, staring. He found that he couldn't speak.

"I think you misspelled 'Reuben,' " Collier said.

Charlie cleared his throat. In a tiny voice he said, "Have you—"

"Yes. I've read it. But no one else has."

What did *that* mean? But before Charlie could figure out a reply, there was a knock at the door. "Officer Collier?" someone called, from the other side.

Collier pushed back his chair. "Time to go."

Charlie stood. He could feel his knees shaking. "Are you taking me to jail?"

"I'm taking you to meet somebody. If the crowd'll let us pass, that is—I think the women in the lobby want to kiss you and the men want you to run for mayor."

Numbly, Charlie held up a hand. "Wait. Wait a minute."

Collier turned to look at him.

"What about the note?" he asked.

"What note?" Collier held his gaze for several seconds, then moved to the door and paused again, his hand on the knob. "The two people, in the lobby. Did you talk to them?"

"What two people?"

"The ones Miller was about to shoot. Girl about your age and a woman in a wheelchair."

"No," Charlie said, "but I think they're okay. The younger lady was crying."

Collier went quiet then. His jaw trembled a little, and he looked down for a moment, as if studying his shoes.

"Officer?"

"I'm fine," Collier said, raising his head. "Those two—the girl and the older lady—are the people I want you to meet."

"Who are they?"

"Rosie and Esther Collier," he said. "Esther's my mother."

Ten years later
6:05 p.m., November 19, 2019

"Not to rush you or anything," Morgan said, "but she's making chili."

Charlie turned on the bench and looked at him through the snow. "She said she and the kids have a Cub Scout deal tonight. She told me to grab a sandwich at the diner near the office."

"The Scout thing was cancelled. And nobody makes chili like Rosie. You know it's true."

Charlie nodded. "I do." He studied his brother-in-law's profile a moment, then let his mind drift back down Memory Lane. Many of those memories began right here.

Charlie Reardon had indeed met Rosie and Esther there in the bank across the street that day—after which they both hugged him and cried some more—and that night they invited him to dinner. Charlie and Rosie were both smitten, from the start. Things progressed steadily from there, and four months later he asked her to marry him. The bride's older brother, Officer Morgan Collier, was best man.

In the years since, Charlie and Morgan rarely talked about what happened that afternoon at First Citizens Bank. Charlie just—what was the word?—compartmentalized it. He'd grown familiar with a lot of mental-health-related terms during the treatment for his PTSD, and although he probably still wasn't completely symptom-free he was at least functional. He had once heard that the best cure for post-traumatic stress is a new kind of stress, and for the past seven years Charlie had been engaged in the low-expertise but high-pressure job of insurance sales. The good thing was, he now had no unpaid debts and no criminal record, so he gave thanks every day for both his new wife and his new life. Charlie Reardon and the former Rosie Collier were the parents of two small boys, and truly happy.

And now, sitting here beside him on a snow-dusted bench, a decade after the interrupted bank heist, Morgan Collier said, out of the blue, "I was told."

Charlie frowned. "What?"

"You asked me once—in fact you've asked me several times, over the years—how I knew to come here to this bank that day, at that particular time. After all, it was on the other end of town from my beat, and from where you and I met that morning. How was it that I showed up here exactly when I did, to find a masked guy who turned out to be Reuben Miller lying comatose in the lobby, and to pick up that bombshell note you dropped on the floor? What was I doing there, only minutes after it all happened? You recall asking me that?"

"I do."

"I mean, let's face it, what were the odds?"

"Pretty long," Charlie said. "Incredible, actually."

"And I never answered you, did I."

"No."

Morgan brushed snow off his cap, sighed, lit another cigarette, and snapped his lighter shut. "Well, I'm answering you now. I was told. I was told, around four-thirty that afternoon, that my mother and sister were here, at First Citizens Bank on Belmont"—he paused and looked up at the building—"and that they were in danger. So I went. Ran a dozen red lights getting here."

Charlie stared at him, scarcely breathing. "Who told you this?"

"A lady named Louise Garrett. She was our neighbor, when I was a kid. Ma said she was some kind of sorceress."

"A what?"

"Ma watched too much TV." Morgan exhaled a plume of blue smoke and watched the wind pull it apart. "But maybe she was right. Louise was also the one who told her that Rosie would meet the love of her life someday. Said Rosie would know it soon as she saw him." He tried a weak grin.

Charlie wasn't grinning. Instead, he said, "Why didn't you tell me before? About this Louise, and what she said to you?"

"Because it sounds crazy, that's why. Think about it. How would this woman from my distant past know what was happening at that moment at a bank five miles away, and know to send me on an errand like that? How *could* she know?"

Charlie stayed quiet awhile, considering that. Then he said, turning the name over in his mind, "I don't think Rosie's ever mentioned a Louise, to me."

"Why should she? The Garretts moved away when we were still kids."

"Away where? Different state?"

"Different neighborhood. They were African American, and times were hard, and remember, this was a long time ag—"

"Louise was black?" Charlie felt a shiver crawl up his spine.

"Yeah. Why?"

Through lips that were suddenly dry, Charlie said, "Anything unusual about her? About the way she looked?" But he thought he already knew.

"Sure was. She wore an eyepatch. Like a pirate." Somehow Morgan managed to chuckle without smiling. "Hell, maybe she *was* a pirate."

And a baseball fan, Charlie almost said. His ears were roaring now, his head spinning.

Both of them fell silent then, lost in their own thoughts. From what seemed a great distance, he heard Morgan apologizing for keeping such a secret, and asking if he was okay. *I'm fine*, Charlie heard himself say. I understand. Which was true. After all, he'd never told anyone about the old woman either, and for the same reason: it was too unbelievable.

When he finally blinked and reconnected to the real world, his brother-in-law had slapped him on the back and was rising from the bench. And was saying something else.

"What?" Charlie asked.

"I said stay here and freeze if you want," Morgan called, over his shoulder. "But I'm hungry. Don't complain if it's all gone when you get home."

Charlie didn't reply. He turned to the bank again, and looked at it in a new light.

I can see more with one eye than most people can with two, she'd said to him.

Maybe she could.

Louise Garrett had not only sent Charlie to keep a crime from being committed and to stop a killer; she had given him the means to save himself. And to—how had she put it?—redirect his path. As a bonus prize, she had sent Officer Morgan Collier to find the damning note and keep too many questions from being asked. Somehow, she had saved all of them.

But the big question remained unanswered. Louise had known ... but *how*? Charlie's past, his personal life, the baseball, his presence in the park, the site of the robbery, the fact that Reuben Miller would be there too, along with Charlie and Rose and Mrs. Collier and then Morgan—

Were there really such things as sorceresses?

Half dazed, Charlie watched the blue Ford pull out into traffic, and raised a hand in response to Morgan's wave. And gradually felt his knotted muscles relax.

Maybe some mysteries weren't meant to be solved. It was time to go home. He rose to his feet, cold and tired but content—at least for now. He was even hungry.

Morgan was right, he thought, and felt himself smile. Nobody made chili like Rosie.

CHANDLER IN THE CLASSROOM

Susan Oleksiw

Alicia dropped the last story manuscript onto Floyd's desk. He always sat in the front row, so he was sure to be noticed when he had a critique of any of her instructions, which was often. It was a wonder she ever got through a class without losing it. Floyd lifted the cover sheet and glanced at the first page of text, where she wrote the grade. His upper lip curled in his usual disdain. The other students did the same and then spent a good three minutes paging through their creative work.

"Today we'll talk about pace and how to use certain techniques to maintain it." She waited while the students opened notebooks and pulled out pens, or flipped open iPads or laptops. A few books slid to the floor, a chair scraped on the linoleum.

It still surprised her how much noise a class of only six students could make. This adjunct gig was going to kill her. The pay was terrible, the students hostile, and the scheduling worse. Maybe she really should consider her brother-in-law's offer to work in his lumber yard—the pay was good, the hours steady, and the office had AC. Out of the corner of her eye she could see Floyd just waiting to pounce.

"Get the dirty deed on the page as early as possible," she said. "That's standard advice." Just then the classroom door banged into the wall. She hadn't closed it, to keep the air circulating in the room, and now wondered if she should have. A young man in a hoodie and jeans slid in.

"This is English 203. Creative Writing."

He scowled at her and slammed the door.

"Your name? The registration period is closed and I've already given the office the final class list."

He glared at the students, who'd turned around to get a look at him. They weren't very interested, but anything was better than being bored. He pulled out a gun.

"Raymond Chandler!" Floyd said. "That's such a cliche."

"It's too small," Randall said. Most of the students ignored Floyd—there was one in every class and he was the one in this one. But Randall enjoyed taking him on. "What you need is a Glock. You should have brought a Glock, man." He turned to the front of the class. "But your point is well taken, Alicia."

"Thank you," Alicia said, but she had her eye on Floyd. He was up to something; she knew it. Maybe she could switch to teaching Romance fiction.

"There's a problem with this technique," Alicia said. "Anyone?"

Carol raised her hand and immediately launched into her favorite topic—cliches. In her view they were the same as vermin—bedbugs, fleas, rats, pythons, all of them.

"Shut up, Lady." The young man waved his gun at her. Undeterred she reached around and pointed at him. "There's no story if the only thing happening is someone acting like a jerk."

"You can't be rude in this class, young man," Alicia said.

"Conflict has to be genuine to make a story work." Carol turned back to the front of the room. "This is such a cliche. Floyd is right."

"You're agreeing with Floyd!" Toby threw his arms out and pretended to be aghast.

The classroom door banged open and one of the security guards took a few steps into the room looking quickly around. The new arrival slid into a chair next to Lenny in the last row, his gun positioned to face him but out of sight of the guard.

Alicia rested her hands on her hips. "If we have one more interruption tonight I may just call the class early and go home."

"Sorry," the guard said, his glance jumping from one student to the other. "Someone got in past security downstairs."

"Well, go find him and leave us alone. Go on!" Alicia waved him out of the room. He left, closing the door behind him.

"All right. You were saying, Carol."

"The plot has to emerge from the characters," Carol said. "The reader doesn't want to feel manipulated."

"I dunno," Lenny said. "I like the idea of a guy with a gun. But not this one." He reached over and pulled the weapon out of the other man's hand. "Now this is so—" He didn't get to say what it was because the other man lunged at him, Lenny's chair tipped over, the two men fell to the floor, and the gun slid to the front of the room. Floyd picked it up.

"I'll take that, Floyd."

Alicia held out her hand—and waited. After a moment, Floyd rested it in her palm just as the new student blundered to the front amidst wails of Watch what you're doing, man. Look out. Hey, that's valuable. The sound of a laptop hitting the floor followed.

"It doesn't look very real," Floyd said.

"That doesn't matter in the movies," Randall said.

"They use real weapons in the movies," Floyd said.

"How do you know?" Carol said.

"They use fake guns on stage," Jennie said, who had a habit of saying the irrelevant.

"Who cares?" Floyd said.

"Lenny, get back in your seat," Alicia said. "You," she said to the new one, "sit down." To stop the squabbling, she banged the butt of the gun on her desk. Eventually, the six—now seven—students restored themselves to their places. The new student began inching forward, changing chairs, until Alicia turned to him.

"I have to have your name." She pointed the weapon at him, holding it sideways. "Or you have to leave." She held the gun loosely in her hand, waving it around to punctuate her statement.

"Sam," he said after a pause.

"What kind of a name is that for a villain?" Toby asked.

"Oh, that's another cliche!" Carol launched into another rant.

Really, they're never going to write anything worth reading, Alicia thought. Maybe I could teach literary fiction.

"More Chandler," Floyd said. "This class is a waste of time."

"Does that mean you're leaving?" Carol perked up.

"Name!" Alicia shouted, trying to regain control of her class.

"I really like all those funny names in Dickens," Jennie said, oblivious to the hubbub around her. "How about Clem Digger? For the new guy?" Floyd guffawed so loud he drowned out the reactions of the others, which were profuse and sometimes profane.

"He has a real name, Jennie. I'm not suggesting naming him." Alicia turned to the young man in question. "Well, what is it?"

"Just Sam," he said, taking in the others.

"Well, Sam, you're not on the list. You can stay for this class but unless the college lets you register for the term, you can't attend again." Alicia rested her hands on her hip, the gun dangling from the index finger on her right hand.

"Okay," Sam said, standing up, which took some time. He was rigid in a crouch. "I'll go. Sorry for the trouble. Can I have my gun?"

"No," Carol said. Everyone turned to look at her. "We haven't settled on whether or not Chandler was right about this. I say he was wrong."

"You're smarter than Chandler?" Floyd started hooting again.

"What kind of gun did Chandler use?" Jennie asked.

"He didn't use a gun, Jennie." Alicia turned to Sam. "Sit down."

"Lenny, you've had your hand up for a while. Do you have something to share?"

"That business about a guy coming in with a gun wasn't meant as advice," Lenny said. Floyd started hooting again. "It was a complaint about artificial plot developments in English mysteries." The room fell silent.

"Um," Sam said. "My gun."

"Lenny, that's very interesting. What have you been reading? The others in the class should check that out."

Lenny rifled through his notes and began reading aloud.

"Boring!" Toby announced.

"What about our stories?" Randall asked. "You're supposed to teach us to write something we can publish."

"What have you published?" Toby tapped Sam on the shoulder. "Come on. Tell us. You got the gun idea from Chandler. Have you sold a story?"

"Just one more fraud," Floyd said.

"Who's a fraud?" Toby charged forward.

"Stop right there!" Alicia stretched out her arm and pointed the gun at Toby. Sam dived under a chair. "No violence. Floyd, this is your last warning. One more outburst like that and you're banned from the class."

"Maybe then we'll get something done," Carol opined.

"It's time for a writing exercise," Alicia said, exhausted. She just wanted to go home. "Choose a method of murder, describe it, and explain why you chose it." She shut her eyes, took a deep breath, and began to pace. "Ten minutes." She repeated this like a mantra, her voice falling to a whisper, for the full ten minutes.

"All right, who wants to read?" Alicia asked. Toby read.

"What's a garrote?" Jennie asked when he finished.

"It's a cliche," Carol said.

Alicia felt another headache coming on. She couldn't seem to get rid of them no matter how many pills she took. Even if she downed a bottle of wine tonight and every night this week, she'd have another headache next week. By the time the students were finished reading and savaging each other's work, it was almost nine o'clock.

"All right. I think that's it for this evening," Alicia said, increasingly frazzled. "And I'd like to point out that no one mentioned the limitations of a gun like this."

"What limitations?" Sam asked.

"Hah! You brought it in and you don't even know?" Toby pulled a face.

"If you run out of bullets you can't hit anyone with it. It's too small to do any damage," Randall said.

"I think it's cute," Jennie said.

"I rest my case," Randall said.

Alicia held the gun in her open palm while Sam inched his chair closer. "It is rather light." She flipped the barrel open. "It's empty too."

"Of course, it's empty," Floyd said. "It's a classroom."

"I don't know why that means it has to be empty," Carol said.

The battle lines were drawn; the students charged.

"I've had enough," Alicia said, but only Sam was listening. "Class dismissed." But no one heard her. The students, except Sam, went on arguing. She repeated herself, a little louder, but still the voices battled on. Then she screamed. "Class dismissed!" at the top of her lungs. At the same time, she held up the gun and to her surprise it went off. The shot echoed around the room; students dived under their chairs. A few scrambled for the exit, with Sam trampling them to be first out the door. Alicia looked up at the hole in the ceiling as plaster rained down onto her face and into her eyes. She sneezed.

"Chandler was right," she said to no one in particular. "It really does get attention."

NAUGHTY OR NICE

Michael Mallory

The boy in the Pennywise the Clown tee shirt and bright green running shoes looked as though the last thing he wanted to do was sit on Santa's lap. Maybe he'd already caught on that Santa was fake news but was afraid to admit it to his mother. At least Roy Talman assumed the attractive, dark-haired woman who was pushing the boy forward was his mother.

Roy didn't believe in Santa, either, except as a paycheck. This was the only job he'd been able to land after getting dumped by the private college at which he'd taught for the past nine years, and there was no question he looked the part: a ruddy face with a snowy white beard (that when last seen was salted chestnut brown), and a beer belly. Roy was 57, but could pass for 70. Acting wasn't required.

Shooting the dark-haired woman a look that he hoped communicated, *My shift is nearly over, so tell your kid to crap or get off the pot*, he saw the boy finally shuffle toward him. The kid was about eight, Roy guessed, and brown-haired, but with the most amazing blue eyes he'd ever seen. He came close enough for Roy to reach down and gently ease him up onto his lap. "Hello, son, what's your name?" he said as merrily as he could at 7:57 in the evening, knowing twelve guys named Sam Adams were home cooling their bubbles.

"Jacob," the boy whispered.

"How old are you, Jacob?"

"Seven."

"All right, Jacob, what would you like Santa to bring you this year?"

The boy said nothing for several seconds, during which time Roy glanced again at the mom, who merely shrugged. Finally Jacob uttered, "Nothing."

"Nothing?" *Nothing will come of nothing*, Roy thought, reciting a line from *King Lear*, which was what he thought he would be doing at the age of 57. "Why not?"

"I don't deserve any Christmas presents."

"Oh, now, Santa doesn't believe that."

"It's true."

Dropping his jolly Santa voice, Roy said, "C'mon, Jacob. Whatever you did that's bothering you, it can't be so bad that you don't deserve a Christmas present."

"It is."

"Look at me, son," he said, gently, and the boy lifted his head and turned those incredible blue eyes on him. "Tell Santa what you did that was so bad."

"You won't be mad?"

"I won't be mad."

Jacob took a deep breath and said, "There was a girl named Suzie who lived next door."

"Okay."

Turning his eyes into fearful lasers, he added, "I killed her."

"The kid said *what*?" Mary Anne Selden, the manager of Slayton's Department Store, shouted.

"That he'd killed his next-door neighbor," Roy repeated. He was now out of his padded red suit and into his street clothes.

"Oh, come on. These are kids, for Chrissake! They're liable to say anything."

"This one didn't strike me as a liar. He seemed genuinely upset."

"We are not paying you to be a child psychologist. We are paying you to say 'Ho ho ho,' and remind the kids to visit the toy section with their parents before they leave."

"Can I at least take a peek at the Nice List?"

"What for?"

"To contact the mom, maybe?"

The "Nice List" was the brainchild of Gene Tuck, the store's marketing director. There were two oversized, ornate books, one labeled "Nice" and one "Naughty," in which the kids could sign in and leave their addresses. Naturally, a few would sign the "Naughty" book, leaving a fake name and address like *Skid Marx, 69 Wetfart Street*, then spend the next week bragging to friends about their wit. Most, of course, put their personal info into the "Nice" book; info which would later be used for direct marketing purposes.

"You're not going to let this drop, are you?" Mary Anne said.

"You weren't there," Roy countered.

"You're right, I wasn't, because I'm not old, fat, or have a white beard."

Wait ten or so years, he thought, but said nothing.

"Look, go talk to Gene about seeing the book if you really must, but whatever you end up doing is all on you. If something goes wrong, it won't splash back on me or the store."

It turned out Gene Tuck was away from his desk, and so was his assistant Darla. But the door was open, which meant Darla had probably stepped out to the bathroom and would be back soon. Roy slipped into Gene's office and went straight to a stack of folio-sized papers that sat on the edge of his desk. Each day's pages of the Nice and Naughty books were taken out so as to have a fresh one the next morning. He quickly searched through the "Nice" pages but found no one named Jacob. He went back and looked for any variation of the name, but still found nothing. Then it hit him: a kid carrying that much self-imposed guilt wouldn't sign in the "Nice" book.

The few "Naughty" book pages were underneath, and there it was: *Jacob Hibbert* and a corresponding address, which Roy committed to memory. As he stepped out of the office, he saw Darla coming in. "Did you need something?" she asked.

"Oh, I was looking for Gene."

"He's at the ad agency today. What do you want?"

"I was, uh ... I wanted to check next week's schedule at the North Pole."

"I have that," Darla said, going to her desk and pulling out a printout. "You're Santa Talman, right? You're scheduled for Tuesday through Friday, afternoon shift."

"I'm not schedule for tomorrow, am I?"

"No, you're off."

"Okay, thanks," he said, turning to leave.

"I wish you guys would write your own schedules down," she muttered behind him.

Roy took advantage of his day off by spending the morning at the public library, where he accessed the local phone book. He was probably the first to do so in this era of smartphones. Looking under *Hibbert*, he found a listing for the Ash Street address he'd committed to memory and jotted the number down on a notepad.

Once home, he waited until 4:00, assuming that Jacob Hibbert would be in school. Then he called. A woman answered the phone. "Mrs. Hibbert?" he asked in his Santa voice.

"No, she's at work," the woman replied.

"Is Jacob there?"

"Who is this?"

"Why, this is Santa Claus." There was a long silence, and then he explained: "My name's Roy Talman and I play Santa at Slayton's Department Store. Jacob came in yesterday and he seemed a little down about Christmastime. I thought maybe I could pep him up a little."

"Santa makes house calls now?"

"Are you his sister?"

"No, I just come over to stay with him until his mom gets home from work."

"I see. Well, if it's not too much trouble ..."

"Hold on."

Roy could hear the sound of the receiver being set down and then the call, "Jacob, phone!" in the background. Over a minute later, the boy's voice came on. "Hello?"

"Hi, Jacob, this is Santa."

"Who?"

"Santa Claus. We met yesterday."

"Are you really Santa or just some guy?"

"That's classified information, I'm afraid." There was a small chuckle at the other end, which Roy took as a good sign. "Jacob, you didn't really mean what you said about killing someone, did you?"

"I did. But I didn't mean to. It did make you mad, didn't it?"

"No, Jacob, I just—"

"Sorry, I have to go now. Bye." He hung up.

After recradling the receiver, Roy went to the fridge for another beer, all the while wondered if he was opening a giant, economy sized can of worms. The last thing he wanted was to provide adverse publicity for the store, particularly the smelly kind that would result from someone misconstruing his interest as Santa Claus stalking a kid. But something about the boy's face and haunted eyes would not leave him.

If Suzie, the girl living next door to the kid, had died, there had to be a record of it. But how could he track it down? Sure, he could contact the police, but he could also imagine how they'd react to Santa Claus reporting a second-degree murder by a second-grade murderer.

"Okay, Roy, think," he admonished himself. *Think* was what he always advised his theatre students by way of preparing for a role.

Back when he had students.

But then as now, it was easier said than done.

Think.

The kid's guilt had seemed as fresh as it was palpable, implying the "murder" must have happened recently. But how would a seven-year-old kill anyone? Obviously, he didn't hit her with a car. Shooting her wasn't impossible, given the plethora of guns and their accessibility even to kids, but it seems like a gunshot would have been detected by the police. Poison? Not impossible, but probably requiring knowledge your average second-grader did not possess. Assuming Suzie was Jacob's age, could he have pushed her out of a tree house?

Hell, did kids still play in tree houses?

Roy had to find out more actual facts about the girl's alleged murder.

It took another beer, his fifth, before he realized how: if Suzie had indeed died, she must have had an obituary in the newspaper.

Picking up the paper, he called the number in the masthead and asked for the obituary department. In a few seconds he was connected to a woman named Kayley Koontz, who asked if he wanted to place a notice.

"No, I need to find out about an existing notice," Roy replied. "At least I'm assuming there would be a notice, if in fact the person really died."

"You don't even know if the person died? Sorry, but you're not making a lot of sense."

Patiently, Roy explained what he was looking for, offering the few details he had.

"My god, you're not talking about Suzie Swift, are you? She was the sister of a friend of mine from high school, and yes, she did die. It was horrible. Let me look up when her notice ran. Hold on." After about twenty seconds, she came back on the line. "The obit ran November 9th under the heading 'Suzanne Alden Swift.' There's a photo of her, too. I think it was her senior picture."

"Senior picture? How old was Suzie?"

"A lot of people wondered about that. Usually you're eighteen when you graduate from high school, but Suzie was some sort of genius, so they kept skipping her ahead. She was only fourteen when she graduated."

Way too young to die, Roy thought, *but also a bit too old to be playing with a second-grader.*

That giant-sized can of worms suddenly threatened to get bigger.

"Are you listening to me, Santa?" a six-year-old girl on Roy's knee whined, having gotten only half-way through her gimme list.

"Huh? Oh, of course! Santa always listens. You want a, uh, a dolly."

"I want a Mulan doll!"

"Right. Anything else?"

Roy could see the line behind her was getting restless. He glanced at the girl's mother, who was standing at the base of the small step unit leading up to Santa's chair, and she picked up on the cue. "Sweetie," the woman said, "why don't you just leave your list with Santa?"

"All right," the girl said. "But it's *Mulan*. Got it?"

"I'll put my best elf on it," Roy said, wearily.

He had a hard time keeping his mind on business throughout the rest of his shift, instead ruminating about Jacob Hibbert and the fate of Suzie Swift. Her obituary, which he tracked down in the library, noted that she had died of an undiagnosed congenital heart condition. Somehow, he had to get in touch with Jacob to tell him Suzie succumbed to natural causes.

After returning home, Roy placed another call to Kayley at the newspaper, expecting to have to leave a message, but she was still there. "You work late," he said.

"I also work in rewrite and that shift ends at nine," she said. "Did somebody else die?"

"No, but I was wondering, since you said you were a friend of Suzie's sister, if you could put me in touch with her."

"This is starting to sound a little creepy."

"All I'm trying to do is help a young boy. If you could pass her number along to me, I'd appreciate it."

"I'll help you on one condition," Kayley said. "If this turns out to be a real story, instead of the fantasy of a crazy kid, you give me exclusive rights to it. I got my journalism degree in June and I'm sick of wasting my time on obits and rewrites. This is something I could take to the editor."

"Agreed," Roy said, hoping he was not letting more worms loose.

"But I'm not going to give you her number. I'll call her, tell her what you want, and if she's interested, she'll call you."

"Agreed again."

Kayley hung up, and nothing happened for another ten minutes. Roy was about to give up hope when the phone rang. "Is this Santa Claus?" a woman's voice asked.

"Is this Suzie Swift's sister?"

"Yes. My name's Heather. Kayley Koontz called and said you wanted to talk to me."

After the obligatory statement of sympathy for her loss, Roy once again explained his quest, after which Heather said, "I know Jacob. He's not a bad kid, but kind of weird. Into horror movies and games, those sort of things. He's an only child, and already kind of a loner. Suzie babysat for him a time or two."

"Do you think Jacob is simply making this up?"

After a few moments of dead air, Heather said, "I really don't know what goes on in the minds of little boys any more than I really know what went on in Suzie's head most of the time. She was on a different planet and hard to relate to. She'd get impatient if you couldn't keep up with her mind, and even most of the teachers couldn't."

"Do you have any information about her heart condition?"

"Only that no one knew she had it."

"Did she have any other health problems?"

Another pause, then: "Look, I don't know you, and I don't know why I should be talking to you, but Suzie was different from everyone in the family. That's all I can say. I wish I could have done something to help her. I should have gotten involved."

"Involved with what?"

"I've already said too much about things I don't really understand. Good night." The line cut off.

I should have gotten involved, Roy thought. What did that mean?

He was still pondering it three beers and a shot later. Heather seemed as though she wanted to tell him something, but was afraid to. But whatever had happened to Suzie Swift, he felt confident it had nothing to do with Jacob Hibbert.

Roy slept later than usual the next day, but awoke feeling rough enough to contemplate calling in sick. If he called now it would give the store enough time to contact Bob Freely, their stand-by Santa, who was genuinely fat, but was also very young. Not only did he have to wear the fake beard and wig, but phony white eyebrows, too. But Roy needed the money, so …

His phone rang and he went to get it.

"Is this Mr. Talman?" a woman on the line asked.

"Yes, who's this?"

"My name is Terri Renella, I'm the roommate of Heather Swift. She said she spoke with you last night."

"That's right."

"I wonder if I'd be able to speak with you as well."

"I'm right here."

"I mean in person. I don't want Heather to overhear."

"I suppose so. When?"

"Today, if possible."

"All right. Where?"

They made plans to meet at a Denny's for early dinner, before she had to go to work.

Lost wages or not, Roy did call in sick, affecting a cough and sniffle as he spoke with Darla. He knew the last thing Marry Anne Selden wanted was a contagious St. Nick.

Leaving the house a bit before the appointed meeting time, he was surprised by the unexpected drop in temperature. It was not yet snowing, but was frigid enough for him to run back inside and break out his heavier coat.

He arrived at Denny's a few minutes early. Terri Renella came in on the dot, taking off her overcoat to reveal hospital whites. "I work in the emergency room of St. Andrew's," she explained. She was small, but conveyed strength. Her brown hair was pulled back into a ponytail, and the fact that she wore no makeup of any kind made her seem even more attractive, like women in Europe. "I'm glad you're taking an interest in Suzie," Terri said, "because no one else has."

"What do you know about all this?"

"Let's order first."

Terri ordered a chicken salad and Roy got the fish and chips and a pint of craft beer. Once their server had gone, Terri began. "Okay, bottom line: I'm pretty sure Suzie was the victim of physical abuse."

"By whom?"

"I can't be certain, but something wasn't right. She didn't have any of the obvious signs, like bruises or the sudden appearance of arm slings, the sort of injuries she'd have to explain away with lies like, 'I walked into a door.' But Heather said she complained of chronic headaches and suddenly had a hard time just staying awake, both of which are symptoms of brain injuries."

"Was she in a car accident?"

"She wasn't old enough to drive, and I never heard about any accident in which she was a passenger. Neither did she play sports, or ride a bike, or any other activity that could potentially lead to a head injury. But there are ways to physically abuse someone and cause those kinds of injuries without leaving any marks."

Terri stopped when the waitress returned with Roy's beer. When it was safe, she went on. "Have you ever killed a fly by bringing your open hand down on as hard as you can?" she asked.

"I've tried, of course. They usually get away."

"If you do the same thing on top of someone's head, you can cause serious damage without leaving any marks. If you do it often enough and hard enough, particularly if you come up behind the person so they can't take defensive steps, it can easily result in brain injury. Brain injuries in turn can lead to heart failure. That's true for anyone, but for a person with an undiagnosed congenital disease, it's a time bomb."

"You think a family member hurt her? A friend?"

"Suzie didn't have friends," Terri said. "I only barely knew her, but it's like she was off on her own planet."

"That's what Heather told me."

"Heather was always a bit overwhelmed by Suzie, who was the family favorite. Heather didn't even go to college because she knew she'd be the lesser student. Now she's enrolled in a tech school, studying to be a dental hygienist. She still feels a little guilty about Suzie's death."

"I got that impression from her, too. Why does she feel guilty?"

"After Heather moved out of the house, and we got our place, Suzie started to reach out to her for the first time in their lives. That's when she started to complain of headaches that were sometimes so bad she couldn't get out of bed. Suzie was trying to prepare for college … at fourteen … but she was having these problems."

Their food came, and the two of them spent the next minute eating in silence. Finally, Roy said, "I really hate to ask this, but is it possible Heather was the one abusing her sister? Maybe out of jealousy or envy?"

"No," Terri replied. "We moved into the apartment nine months ago, and Suzie's calls didn't start until six or seven months later. Besides, Heather simply isn't capable of that sort of violence."

"Do you know if Suzie ever mentioned Jacob Hibbert in those calls?"

"Not that I heard. Look, you say that Jacob told you he killed Suzie, but I can't imagine why he would think that, unless it was a reaction to a dream so vivid that he can't tell it from reality. Some people have that problem. But Jacob's, what … seven? He couldn't possibly hit her hard enough to cause the damage."

"That narrows it down a bit, doesn't it?"

"It does. I can't prove anything, but I have a feeling I know where the abuse was coming from. I'm taking a chance telling you this, because Heather told it to me in strictest confidence. Everybody always commented on how different Suzie was from the rest of the family, in looks and in other ways. Finally, she got suspicious enough to confront her mother about it."

"She was adopted?" Roy asked.

"She was illegitimate. Suzie's real father was a guy her mom worked with at the time. Her dad ... at least the man she thought was her dad ... had no idea until he overheard the confrontation. I probably don't have to state that he did not take it well. He drinks a lot, so he's not always pleasant to be around anyway. Suzie's last call left Heather genuinely upset. She didn't want to talk about the details, but kept saying, 'How dare he?' Suzie died the next day."

"Oh, lord," Roy uttered, starting to wish he'd left well enough alone.

Half-way through Roy's shift the next day, Mary Anne Selden appeared at the "North Pole" to tell him that he was needed in the toy shop. Nothing like this had ever happened before, and many of the kids and mothers in line reacted with disappointment, and even a few tears. "Don't worry, folks," Mary Anne announced, "Santa will be back in just a few minutes. Please bear with us."

Roy remained in character as he walked through the store to Mary Anne's office, where a woman was waiting. "What's this about?" he asked.

"This customer came to complain about the smell of alcohol on you," Mary Anne said.

"What? No, that's wrong. I never drink before a shift."

"Take a whiff for yourself if you don't believe me," the customer said.

Mary Anne leaned close to Roy's chest, made a face, and said, "Yes, I see what you mean. Mr. Talman, you are no longer working for Slayton's. You knew we had a zero-tolerance policy for drinking when you took the job."

Roy tried protesting again, but then detected the scent of liquor on his Santa suit himself. "I ... I don't ..."

"Hang up your costume and leave at once," Mary Anne said. "Your last check will be mailed to you."

Realizing there was little use in arguing further, Roy made his way to the makeshift dressing room, where he saw Bob Freely putting on the finishing touches to his makeup. "Bad luck, man," Freely said, with a smile.

"Bullshit is the word I'd use," Roy spat. "Wait, how come you already knew? I got canned less than two minutes ago." Then it hit him. "You son of a bitch, you poured booze in my costume to get me fired!"

"Look, all's fair in love, war, and steady employment," Freely told him. "What's more, you can't prove I did anything."

Roy's fists clenched. He wanted to lay the fat bastard out right then and there but two things prevented him: one was that it would land him in even deeper trouble with the store, and the other was that he'd always been terrible in a fight. Instead he changed and left.

On the way home it started to snow. Roy knew he was out of beer at home and considered stopping to get some. After all, if he was going to be fired for drunkenness, he might as well live down to the charge. Passing his local liquor store, he slowed down and turned on his blinker to turn in, but then muttered, "Bullshit" and kept going. He wouldn't give Mary Anne and Freely the satisfaction. Maybe what he'd give them instead is a wrongful termination suit against Slayton's.

Roy was cleaning up after dinner—a ham steak and two eggs—when his phone rang. It was Jacob Hibbert. "How did you find my home number?" Roy asked him.

"My babysitter wrote down the name you gave her when you called here, and I found your number in the phone book. I'm calling because I think something's going on next door. I heard a lot of yelling, even with the windows closed. Then I saw Mrs. Swift come out and get into the car and drive away. That was a couple hours ago. Then their dog started howling, and he usually doesn't."

"Have you told your folks?"

"My mom's out at her book club meeting and my dad goes bowling on Thursdays."

"Who's watching you?"

"Our other neighbor's daughter is here, but she's upstairs in the bathroom talking on the phone with her boyfriend. I think something's wrong next door, but I didn't do it."

"Look, Jacob—"

"Amber's out of the bathroom now. I have to go."

"Jacob, wait," Roy said, but the boy had already hung up.

"Christ."

Calling the police seemed pointless, since the best he could offer was that he heard a rumor from a second-grader about something that might have happened in a different part of town. If anyone called the cops, it should be Heather, as a family member. But how could he contact her? Sure, the boy managed to find him, but he had a landline, and was in the book. Like most other young people, Heather probably only had an unlisted cell. "Think, dammit, *think*!" Then he shouted, "Terri!"

Punching in 411, he asked for the number of St. Andrew's Hospital and was automatically connected. Starting with the general operator, he asked for Terri by name, and began the agonizingly long ladder crawl up to the nurse's station in the ER.

"Terri hasn't come in yet," the woman at the other end told him. "Can I take a message?"

"This is a personal emergency," Roy said. "Tell her she has to call Heather, and

Heather has to call the police. There's trouble at Heather's house. Is that clear?"

"Are you calling for an ambulance?"

"I'm calling for Terri Renella! She has to contact Heather Swift, her roommate, and—"

"Why don't I simply call her at home then?" the nurse asked.

"Great idea. When you get her, tell her to call this number." Roy rattled off his mobile number, a flip-top "geezer" phone that he rarely used and hoped was charged up.

After getting on his coat, he checked the phone and found one lone bar. "Good enough," he said, starting out for his car. Half-way to Ash Street (and hoping he remembered the address correctly), it rang. "Terri?" he said into it.

"This is Heather. What's going on?"

"Jacob heard an argument at your place and saw your mom storm out and drive away, and now he says the dog's howling like a banshee."

"Nessie never howls."

"That's the point. You need to call the police and then get there right away. I don't know what's going on, but it sounds like something's wrong."

Then Roy's phone died.

"*Christ!*"

It was snowing harder by the time he got to the Hibbert home. No one else was there yet. He got out of his car to wait for whoever showed first. He could hear the dog howling, though it barely sounded canine, more like the low, mournful cry of a human exhausted from sobbing. Within minutes, he heard a siren, and before long a police cruiser pulled up to the curb in front. Two officers, one a middle-aged guy with a moustache and the other a young African American woman, got out. Running to them, Roy introduced himself to the male officer, whose nametag read "Weybourne," and said, "The woman whose folks own this house isn't here yet, but I got a call from the little boy next door about a loud argument and the dog howling."

"Who's inside?" Officer Weybourne asked.

"I don't know." Then another car pulled up and Roy saw Terri Renella and another young woman, who looked like a bundled-up child, get out. "Roy," Terri called, "this is Heather."

"What's happened?" Heather Swift asked.

"Do you have a key to the house, ma'am?" Weybourne asked.

Fighting her way through her heavy down coat to her jeans pocket, Heather fished it out and handed it to him.

"Is the dog going to be a problem?" the policeman asked.

"No, he's a border collie and very sweet. He never howls like this."

"Okay, stay back, please." As the two officers walked onto the porch, the woman, whose tag ID'd her as Jackson, placed her hand over the grip of her gun but left it holstered.

Then a voice from behind them called, "Is that you, Santa?" Turning, Roy saw Jacob on the front porch of his house, with no sitter in sight. He was wearing pajamas.

"Jacob, go back inside!" Roy shouted.

Officer Weybourne pounded on the door of the house and shouted, "Police, open up." There was no answer. Before using the key, he tried the door and found it unlocked. Opening it slowly, he jumped back from a dark flash that ran past him and into the yard. It was Nessie, who jumped into Heather's arms.

The officers went inside the house. Moments later, Jackson re-emerged and ran to the prowl car. Roy could hear her call over the radio for an ambulance.

"Who is it?" Heather cried.

Now Officer Weybourne came out. "Ma'am, I'm sorry, but I'm going to have to ask you to come in here and tell me who it is." Handing the dog to Terri, Heather followed the policeman inside. A cry soon pierced the night, and soon Heather staggered back onto the porch as though in a trance.

"Honey, are you all right?" Terri called, as Nessie jumped away from her and ran toward Heather.

"I ... don't know," Heather called back, sinking onto a front step. "My father ... so much blood."

Terri gently picked Heather up off the step and led her to her car, while Nessie trotted behind them, ignoring the dusting of snow. Terri opened the door and helped Heather get seated inside, and then caressed and kissed her face in such a way that made Roy realize they were more than roommates.

Roy felt a tugging on his coat, looked down, and saw Jacob, still in nothing but pajamas and slippers. "Something's happened, hasn't it?" the boy asked.

"Jacob, what are you doing out here in the cold?" Roy said.

"I'm okay," Jacob said, but he was shivering. Roy took off his own coat and draped it around the boy, who added, "I didn't do it this time."

"You didn't do it the other time, either."

"Jacob, stay here," Roy said, then made his way through the cold to the car in which Terri and Heather sat. "Is she all right?" she asked.

"She's in shock," Terri said.

Officer Jackson was now moving back toward the house and Roy ran to her. "What happened to him?" he asked.

"I'm not the M.E.," the policewoman replied, "but it looks like suicide with glass from a broken bottle. Sir, we need you to stay back, all right?"

As Roy moved back to the small, bundled figure of Jacob, a girl came out onto the porch of the Hibbert residence and shouted, "There you are, you little brat! Get back here!"

"I want to talk to Santa Claus first," Jacob called back.

"Don't be such an idiot!"

Roy spun around. "The boy said he wants to talk to me, dammit!" he yelled in a theatrical voice that was heard at the end of the block.

The babysitter went back inside.

Roy knelt down to face Jacob. "She probably didn't mean it when she called you a brat."

"Yes, she did," the boy said. "Sitters don't like me. Suzie used to call me a lot worse than 'brat.' I didn't like her, either. That's why I …"

"Jacob, listen to me. You did not kill Suzie."

"I did! The last time she came over she fell asleep, and when I woke her up she said I'd better not tell my mom and dad that she was sleeping. Then she called me dumb and said I'd still be in second grade when I was fourteen, and I got so mad I …"

"You did what?"

"I made a voodoo doll of her. I saw it in a movie. I found one of her hair bands at the house and it had a piece of her hair in it. I wrapped it around an old beanbag doll and wrote her name on it, and then stuck a pin through its chest. Then she died."

"Jacob, if you can't listen to me, listen to Santa. Suzie died of heart disease. It had nothing to do with you."

"But I stabbed the doll in the heart!"

"Son, how about we go back to your house and talk about it there. I'm getting cold."

The ambulance was now pulling up in front of the house without its siren wailing. There was no need, since the EMT's had been informed that Heather's father was already dead.

Jill Swift swooned at the police station when told her husband, Denny Swift, was dead. Fortunately, she was sitting down at a table in the interview room. She had finished telling the police about her violent argument with Denny, who was extremely drunk and threatening to hit her with an empty bourbon bottle. She managed to wrench the bottle out of his hands, causing him to respond by smacking her on the top of the head with an open hand. Then he told Jill he'd keep doing it until she was dead, like Suzie. Calling her a whore, he raised his hand again, and this time she put her arms over her head for protection, not even conscious that she still held the bottle.

The next thing Jill remembered was getting into her car and speeding off to the police station. She had no recollection of the bottle shattering from Denny's blow above her head, nor the fact that a jagged spire of glass had sliced through his wrist, gashing the radial artery, causing him to bleed to death. When Jill was finished at the stationhouse, she was driven to the emergency room, where the doctors found no fractures or other serious injuries … at least not physical ones.

Kayley Koontz was the first to get the story out, though at Roy's insistence, neither he nor Jacob was mentioned by their real name. Roy didn't want Jacob to become a *cause celebre*, and he didn't want any notoriety to interfere with his North Pole duties, since two weeks before Christmas he'd been called back to work with a surprisingly heartfelt apology from Mary Anne Selden. They needed him because a newly-installed security camera recorded Bob Freely planting a joint into the pocket of the new swing Santa's red coat. Feely was not only dismissed, he was escorted out of the store by the police.

The swing Santa in question was a bearded retiree named Phil Cohen, who was new to performing, so Roy did what he could to help him prepare for the role. One day as Roy was changing out of his costume, Cohen said, "I'm so glad you taught me all about really listening to what the kids are saying, because I had a real interesting customer yesterday, a little guy named Jacob, with the bluest eyes I've ever seen. He said he felt better now and wanted a Christmas present after all, whatever that meant. He asked for a zombie apocalypse. At first I thought he meant he wanted Armageddon to happen, but I finally figured out he meant a video game. Boy, what these kids are watching today."

"It's a different world than when we were young," Roy said.

"Yeah, but at least he still believes. I mean, he must, since he told me I was a really good Santa, but he liked the real one better, the one who helped him when he needed it."

"Oh, that one," Roy Talman said, smiling through his bushy white beard.

CHAIN OF HEARTS

J.T. Siemens

The stolen bunny ornament fell from Kitt's overcoat. Picking the trinket off the floor, I looked into her green eyes as I handed it back. They seemed to spark playfully under the red glow of the Christmas lights outside the window.

Oops. The bunny disappeared back inside her coat and she took a sip of her rum toddy.

I told her I recalled that particular critter from the tree at the Pan Pacific. Across the table, Rachel and Eddie laughed.

Rachel, our matchmaker, called Kitt a naughty little klepto, and Eddie, Rachel's fiancé, asked her what else she had jacked that night.

After a quick deliberation, she shrugged, took another sip, and reached back inside her coat. Turned out the night's haul consisted of tree ornaments: a scowling green Grinch, *(Fairmont),* a pink-and-blue plastic LED icicle *(Hotel Georgia),* a miniature snow globe *(Four Seasons),* a micro-menorah *(Sutton Place),* a Rasta-Jesus *(Pac Rim),* and a blue sheep wearing a Santa cap *(unknown).* Kitt's booty sat in the middle of the table, an eclectic assemblage chronicling our jaunt through the holiday bedecked lobbies of the city's upscale hotels. We marveled that none of us had witnessed any of the acquisitions.

Asking the origin of the blue sheep, I said I didn't recall seeing it on any of the trees.

Greek place I popped into before meeting you guys. Needed a warm-up.

We howled and ordered another round.

On our second date, Kitt kipped silverware from an Italian joint on Main. As we walked down the street I asked why.

Why what?

Why did you steal the cutlery? It wasn't even especially nice.

Why is the sky blue, Jack?

I took out my phone and asked Google. When I began blathering about atmospheric molecules scattering blue light, she pulled the filched fork and jabbed me in the ass.

Ow.

The sky's blue because the sky's blue, Jack. It spoils the fun to question everything. Just do or don't do.

It sounded like some sort of half-baked zen koan, but I got the gist: Kitt does what Kitt does. Later that night, we played pool and shared a pitcher. She kicked my ass three for three, and on our way out she purloined three red-feathered darts from the board near the door. As she nonchalantly pocketed them, I couldn't help but jerk my head around.

Her excuse was that the beer was overpriced and we had to make up our losses somehow. Seemed a good enough reason. I liked it better than the sky is blue crap.

Out on the street we had an impromptu game of darts. As a target, we used a poster advertising amateur stripper night on the side of a boarded-up building. First one to hit the dancer's tits won. Kitt won.

Wanting to keep the night going, we wound up at an old-school diner on Granville, sipping coffee and talking, me providing the bulk of the conversation. I told her my story: city boy, schooled at McGill, sucked at sports, one serious girlfriend years ago, found work in a bank, where I met my friend, Rachel. I confessed that the only thing I ever stole was a Mars bar from the corner store when I was eight. My mom found out and made me take it back and apologize.

Her eyes lifted to mine as she sipped her coffee. *Nice story, Jack.*

Intrigued by her thieving ways, I asked her about the first thing she ever stole.

A chain of hearts. Appearing suddenly impatient, she tossed a tenner on the table. *C'mon, let's go for a drive.*

Kitt worked as a sales rep for a local microbrewery and got to drive the company van, the side panel depicting a mural of a killer whale breeching in a sea of sudsy beer. We drove around for a while listening to the *White Stripes*. She sang her heart out on every track.

You're a good singer.

She stopped singing. *What?*

YOU'RE A GOOD SINGER!

She glanced over, smiling, eyes all soft. She blew me a kiss. Just like that, Kitt added another heart to her chain.

Then I helped her boost a manhole cover at Pender and Abbott, thing must've weighed three hundred pounds.

Back in the van, she pulled off her jeans and rode me on the passenger seat. I thought my head was going to explode from my body like a rocket.

Next day at the bank, Rachel noticed a bounce in my step. *You got action last night.*
Yup.
Her place or yours?
Her work van.
Interesting.

Christmas came and went. Neither Kitt nor I had any family nearby, so we went on a sort of holiday tear. Boxing Day was ideal because stores were jammed; the clerks too busy helping customers to notice a light-fingered pixie grabbing whatever doodads she fancied. I like to think we appeared as any normal couple, the bored yet dutiful male tagging along behind his girl. Only in my case, the affected boredom was pure acting; inside, my heart was a snare drum and rivers flowed from my pits. I felt obscenely giddy, to the point of nearly passing out several times in stores.

The real fun was that I never knew if or when she was about to pinch an item. We could wander into half a dozen shops and she wouldn't lift a thing. Then we'd be in a department store, and *boom,* she'd walk out wearing sunglasses I hadn't even seen her slip on. It was like she wore a cloak of invisibility, or exuded a sufficiently casual vibe to fly completely beneath clerk radar.

Kitt's proclivity wasn't limited to malls or stores. One time she shadowed me into the men's room of a bar. I assumed she was horny, but then she pulled out a screwdriver and pried the condom dispenser from the wall. Leaving the bar, Kitt waved to the bartender while packing the white metal case full of prophylactics under her arm, coins jingling inside.

In the parking lot, I informed her I had plenty of protection at home.

She laughed and set the condom dispenser down by a dumpster and we drove away.

Back at my place, she took a look around.
You have almost nothing. I like it.
It's because I knew you were coming. I hid anything of value.
She kissed me. *I already own the most valuable thing here.*

The next morning, I realized Kitt had lifted a pair of cufflinks that had been a gift from my mother. I smiled. Far as I was concerned, she could take it all.

When I expressed an interested in seeing her digs, she told me her place was a disaster. I didn't doubt it, but I still wanted to see it. Morbid curiosity, I guess.

Kitt spent many nights at my place. Aside from a toothbrush, she never left anything behind. No yoga pants in my sparsely appointed closet, no Tampax in my near empty cupboards. I am a minimalist, a fan of clean lines and empty space. When I have my own office at the bank, my desk will be a clear open plain where anything is possible.

Around the cusp of spring, something changed. I began waking in the middle of the night with cold sweats, and my days were tinged with a sense of dread. I came down with a bitch of a cold. One day at work I stood at my till listening to some geezer bitch about his monthly service fee when Kitt swirled through the door in her overcoat. She took a place in line and waited patiently, sweet smile distracting me. Eventually the geezer tottered off and Kitt slid into his place.

So this is where you work. Very stark. I can see why it appeals to you.

It's a bank, I said, *pretty standard.* I glanced around. Except for pens and RRSP pamphlets, and maybe the PIN console at each till, there was nothing to casually walk off with. Still, I motioned with my eyes toward the overhead cameras. Surely she wouldn't try anything in a bank.

Kitt reached into her tote and handed me a to-go container of soup. *Chicken noodle: for your cold.*

Just then, Rachel walked past in the background and looked up.

Kitt!

Rach!

The ladies embraced, leaving me awkward at the till while they gave a hurried exchange. *Let's get caught up soon ... coffee ... drinks ... whateves ... 'kay call you later.* Kitt blew me a kiss and was off. Just before the door, she grabbed a random umbrella from the stand and smiled at security on her way out. What the heck, everyone takes umbrellas. It's practically not even stealing.

For a short time, Kitt appeared to be cutting back. We went out to entirely theft-free dinners, to movies where she paid for tickets. She brought me to one of her work functions where she lit up the room with her charm while serving samples of the latest Pilsner and Hefeweizen. I drank a bit too much brew and didn't eat enough, but I gave a buzzy grin when she introduced me as her beau to several of her co-workers.

Just another normal couple, I thought, considering the logistics of bringing Kitt home to meet the parents in Ontario. I wondered if there was a pill she could take to prevent her from robbing them blind, or if she could simply will herself not to. I strongly doubted the latter. My mother was a fastidious yet ferocious collector of little figurine-crap, bunny and otherwise. She'd spot a bare doily straight away.

The wee hours found the two of us having a nightcap in Mango Cove, a local watering hole. I brought up the whole meet the parents idea.

Kitt looked like she had a sudden case of heartburn. I asked if it was too soon.

Much. But there's something I really *need, Jack. I need that bear.*

Huh?

With an uptick of her chin, she gestured toward the entrance, where a massive, sombrero-wearing polar bear stood on its hind legs. Under the muted bar lights, the creature looked real. It was certainly big enough.

Is that thing stuffed?

Made in China. Totally hollow inside. Corona reps give them to bars that push their piss-water. I've had my eye on that bear for a long time and I want it.

I really don't see how. Thing's ten feet tall.

Almost eleven actually. She threw some money down on the table. Always cash, never plastic. She never stiffed a server, and claimed she'd never ripped off a library book.

She headed for the bear. *C'mon, Jack.*

I rose, assessing the scene. The restaurant was cavernous and maybe a quarter full, with most of the wait staff taking orders. The bored-looking bartender watched sports highlights on the big screen.

Kitt was already tipping the bear backward, looking comically diminutive beside it. *You take the legs. It's awkward, but it's light.* Heart hammering and adrenaline fizzing, I picked the bear up by its hind legs, and began backing toward the entrance.

She tugged the other direction. *No, Jack, we go through the kitchen. Why do you think I parked in the alley?*

And that's how we waltzed out of the restaurant with an eleven-foot polar bear, going right past a stoner busboy who actually held the door for us. Wrestling the bear down the metal staircase into the alley, she warned me to keep my head down on account of the camera on the wall.

The bear's prohibitive length prevented closing the rear doors of the van. We drove off, ass end of the bear sticking out the back. She turned on the stereo and began belting out R.E.M.'s *Losing my Religion*. I had a flash of getting canned by the bank over a conviction for stealing a stupid goddamn bear. I turned off the stereo. *What if we got caught, Kitt?*

We didn't. I doubt the camera even works in that dump, but it's still a good idea to steer clear for a while. How high is the ceiling in your place, by the way?

Over the next few weeks, I attempted to rein in Kitt's more impulsive urges. Knowing I could never hope to eliminate her compulsion, I merely sought to direct it somewhat. I steered her away from the high-end shops where clerks stink-eye you the moment you enter. No electronics, no jewelry, no cosmetics. For a short time, it worked, and there were maybe three days of relative calm. Then suddenly she snatched an iguana (*it was a rescue, Jack!*) from a pet store in the mall. When I gave her a hard time about it, she grew sullen and resentful and commenced snatching random objects at a furious pace. A scarf from Nordstrom's, one hundred red helium balloons, blocks of gouda, razors, a jackhammer from a construction site, and three stuffed penguins (no doubt to provide Antarctic juxtaposition to the polar bear, who, thanks to my vaulted ceiling, had taken up residence in the corner of my living room).

I still hadn't been to Kitt's place. After assisting the snaffle of several boxes of Nutella from a loading dock behind Whole Foods, I asked her if she even *had* a place.

Of course, I have a place.
When am I going to see it?
Wait till I uh ... purge some stuff.
You're a hoarder, aren't you?
I'm not *a hoarder, Jack. I'm also not a fan of labels. I think we should maybe give some of this Nutella to homeless people. It's full of calories, and so delicious. What say you?*
I say we need a break, Kitt.
I thought you were having fun.
I keep feeling something bad is going to happen. I haven't slept in a month and it's making me mental. I can't keep doing this. I'm sorry.

Kitt's face fell. She tore open one of the boxes and handed me a jar of Nutella. *Me too, Jack.*

I walked away down the slushy street, feeling sick. I wanted to turn to see if she was watching, but I tossed the Nutella in the garbage and hopped on a bus at Marine Drive, not caring the destination.

Next day at the bank, Rachel pulled me aside. *Kitt has a criminal record for theft; a lengthy one. I talked to my cop cousin. They're not supposed to look into people's records, but they do. He said if she gets busted again, she'll do time.*

I said it didn't matter; it was over between us. Rachel didn't believe me.

Over the next few weeks, I nearly called Kitt dozens of times. I saw that she had tried calling me three times but had left no message. She had a thing about the number three. There wouldn't be a four.

At a craft fair in April, I went looking for a gift for my mom's birthday. Maybe a purse, I thought, or some organic hippy soap. I was sniffing a sachet of some lavender potpourri junk, thinking my mom might like it. There was a long line of customers and only one lady taking money. Without thinking, the sachet fell into my coat pocket, rewarding me with a gush of pleasure.

I looked up. There she was. Kitt. Smiling from twenty feet away, beside a kiosk selling religious ornaments. She held a sparkly gold crucifix in her hand and then, *poof,* it vanished. My high roared back, more potent than ever.

Kitt gave her smile and a confirming nod, telling me she knew *exactly* what I was feeling.

That damn smile.

Ten seconds later we stood face to face.

Hi, Jack.

Hi, Kitt.

Not stalking me or anything, are you?

I could ask the same.

We smiled.

She asked me out for coffee and I told her it was too late in the day for coffee.

Beer?

Sure.

Snaking her arm through mine, we meandered through the artisan booths. It was like we'd never been apart. That's how it was with us.

At the exit, Kitt was first out the door. She smiled over her shoulder at me and then her face tightened in alarm. I looked back to see a beast of a security guard lumbering forward, eyes fixed on Kitt.

I turned, blocking the beast with my back.

Her panicked eyes searched mine. I grabbed the crucifix from her pocket and pushed her away, told her to run. She bolted, just as the beast grabbed my shoulder, trying to shove past. I struggled with him long enough for her to escape. My shirt tore. He called me a dumbass, dragged me to the security office, and called the cops.

Three hours later, I found Kitt leaning against her work van, parked across the street from the police station.

You are a dumbass, Jack.

So I've been told.

Did they charge you?

Yes, but I'm going to plead temporary insanity, or work some sort of Stockholm Syndrome angle.

I guess this means I've got to show you my place now.

Least you could do.

Kitt drove through the streets, making her way east through the city. She wasn't singing. A light rain fell, even though the sun was bright and there was not a cloud in the blue blue sky. I felt an almost nirvanic serenity. She looked over at me. Those eyes. Man, they got me every time.

We were driving past the mall when she commented on my torn shirt.

I think we should get you a new one.

I nodded.

She pulled into the mall's underground parking lot. *New shirt, and then we'll go straight home. I promise.*

She parked near the elevators and we got out. I couldn't stop smiling. 🔫

GINA'S GREATEST HITS

Lina Chern

Gina sat in the back office of her Aunt Josie's bar, waiting to get her ass chewed by her Uncle Wayne. She'd gotten nabbed by the cops for getting into a fistfight with Kaczmarek, the douche bag neighbor. Fist-fight was maybe not the best word for what happened, which was that Gina had clobbered Kaczmarek in the face with a snow shovel and shattered his nose.

The office was a hot, tiny room with an old wooden drawer desk and a crud-covered window facing Damen Avenue. Gina sat in the wobbly chair where they put busboys to fire them. Josie's old-lady perfume choked the room, and Gina wished she could open the window, but it was nailed shut and blocked by a clanking radiator. A boxy Ukrainian Jesus glared down at her from the wall. Gina made a face at Him and turned away to stare at a ceramic paperweight: a boy and girl with huge, sappy eyes, sailing a wooden boat stuffed with farm animals. Gina cocked her head. Were the kids taking the animals on vacation? Another one for the list, Gina thought. *Never clutter up your place with knickknacks and then complain that you have too much crap.*

Uncle Wayne opened the door and a sliver of mid-afternoon bar noise slipped in with him—glass and soft voices. McGreevy, the cop who had dropped Gina off, was at the bar sipping one of Josie's espressos from a tiny white cup. He looked like he was at a doll tea party.

"You want a Coke or something?" Uncle Wayne sat down across from her in the boss's chair. He was not really her uncle. There was no keeping track of all the second and third cousin-ships and once-removals of her mom's huge Ukrainian-Italian family. They were all just "uncles," all the loud guys who ran the bar and gambling room Aunt Josie had inherited from old Uncle Vito years ago. The gambling room was in the back of the bar, behind a pale, scuffed door marked ELECTRICAL.

Gina shook her head no to the Coke.

"What'd you break that shithead's face for?" Uncle Wayne said. He was six and a half feet solid, and over 300 pounds. All the Dios, men and women, were either tall, fat or both, though Wayne was the opposite of what people meant when they called you fat. They meant you were stupid, lazy, slow. Uncle Wayne was slow, maybe, but slow like one of those jungle cats on a nature special.

Gina glanced up at him. "I thought McGreevy told you what happened."

"*Officer* McGreevy did tell me." Wayne settled back in the chair. "And now I'm asking you."

Gina's snow boots had left sludge on the floor, and she scuffed at it with her toe. "Mom and I shoveled out a space in front of the house. It took like an hour. We got up at four." It had snowed all night and the drifts were waist high. They had looked to Gina like warm pillows she could sink into and go back to sleep.

"Was your dad with you?"

"No. Mom said to let him sleep because he was up late the night before." *Getting shitfaced*, she didn't add, but understanding flickered across Wayne's face anyway. "She put a chair down when she left for work." You shoveled out a parking space, you put down a chair to mark it. Everybody knew that. "But then Kaczmarek just moved the chair while she was at work, and took her space. She tried to say something to him." Gina felt the rage slice through her again. "She wasn't even rude or anything."

Wayne tilted his head. "And then?"

"He got mad and said some stuff." He was going to make her say it, wasn't he?

"What stuff?"

Gina stared back at Wayne. "He called her a fat dago cunt." She didn't remember exactly what happened next. She just remembered the look on her mom's face, a sad sort of agreement: *yep, that's me*. The rest was lost in a white-hot gap. It wasn't even Kaczmarek she was mad at, Gina realized, with his stupid slicked-back hair and Cavariccis. It was her mom. Gina was mad that her mom could hate herself so much. That she would recognize herself in those ugly words.

"Well, you almost landed in some deep shit." Wayne picked a pencil out of a red plastic cup. "McGreevy was supposed to be off today." McGreevy was practically on staff at the bar. He stopped by weekly to pick up the suitcase Aunt Josie left tucked for him under the very desk in front of Gina. *Let me get this straight*, the grizzled old cop had drawled, shuffling his feet in the dirty snow on the curb and sucking his teeth. *You wanna press charges?* His dead blue eyes fixed on Kaczmarek. *Go on record you got your ass beat by a thirteen-year-old girl? Be glad to set you up*. He had his hand on Gina's shoulder. He was either trying to comfort her or keep her from ripping the rest of Kaczmarek's face off.

Gina still couldn't tell if Wayne was mad at her or not. "My dad already yelled at me," she said helpfully.

Wayne's sharp eyes wandered over her, and she knew he was looking for bruises. It was *complicated*, Francine said to anyone who made the mistake of asking. *My husband's relationship with the kids is complicated.* Gina thought it was actually very simple. Jake was not her real dad, and so he did not love her the way he loved Kyle and Jenny. No skin off her ass. Her half-brother and -sister actually had it tougher. They never knew which Jake they were going to get: giggling, wrestling-on-the-floor-in-pajamas Jake, or red-faced, shouting-when you-spilled-juice Jake. At least Gina knew the son-of-a-bitch hated her. She'd figured it out years ago after watching Jenny climb into Jake's lap, seeing him smother her with cuddles and kisses. She had tried to do the same, but she did not get cuddles and kisses. She got a lit cigarette in her elbow. That was the last time she made the mistake of trying to love him.

"What did your dad say?" Uncle Wayne asked.

Gina didn't roll her eyes because she knew Wayne hated it. "He said I needed to find a better way to solve problems than with my fists." *Look whose cow is mooing*, went one of Josie's batty old Ukrainian proverbs. Jake could be a regular choir boy when it suited him. Which was any time he wanted to pick on Gina. *He didn't have to adopt you*, Fran would say. *Not every man would adopt another man's kid.* Big whoop. Gina knew Jake had only married Fran because he'd knocked her up with Kyle when Gina was three. Now Jake was stuck with another guy's bastard kid and two of his own. *Never have sex without rubbers.* Gina didn't pay much attention in health class, but she'd heard this lesson loud and clear, and put it on her list. She kept a running tally in her head of things to avoid when she grew up, all the crappy choices adults made and then wondered how their lives got so fucked up. Sort of like the Ten Commandments, but there were a lot more than ten, so instead of the big stone tablet from the Sunday school books, Gina imagined a set of glowing pages flipping past. Like the song list in Josie's old-fashioned jukebox. The Greatest Hits.

Fran had apparently not heard the one about sex without rubbers. Her folks went full Italian and tossed her out after she got pregnant with Gina at sixteen. She'd stayed in Ukrainian Village, so at least the rest of the family could drop in with a tray of lasagna, or stay with Gina when Fran had to work late. All that changed when Fran met Jake, with his oily smile, raggedy Members Only jacket and his union trucking gig that he talked about like he owned the company. *He* was going to be the one to take care of them now. Or so he said. Jake's version of "taking care" consisted of pissing off

Fran's family until they didn't come around anymore. And also stealing. He couldn't go into a store without pinching something—a lighter here, a pack of cigarettes there. The worst part was when he slipped stuff into Jenny and Kyle's pockets. He'd tried it with Gina and she shut him down quick—another reason she was on his shit list.

It all worked okay for a few months, maybe a year, at a time. Then Jake would get busted for lifting a cartload of TV's and trying to sell them at the flea market with all the other scumbag thieves. Fran would have to go on food stamps, and they would eat ketchup sandwiches for dinner until Jake convinced his parole officer he was a changed man. Then the whole cycle would start over again. Gina imagined a record stuck on repeat, the same song squawking out of the jukebox over and over. *Never depend on anyone else to take care of you.* Fran was still working at the bar where she met Jake, one of those women people either laughed at or didn't see at all. Younger than her tired face made her look. Wearing too much makeup and a feathered hairstyle ten years out of date. No one knew she could do a dead-on Mickey Mouse voice, and that she always said the right thing when you were upset. No one knew she made pancakes that were soft inside and just a little bit crunchy outside, whenever she could get her hands on some eggs. No one knew her hugs smelled like lemons and soap.

The ceramic kids blurred in Gina's eyes, as if their boat had drifted into a thick fog. "It's not fair," Gina whispered.

"Are you sorry?"

Wayne's voice startled her and she blinked up at him. She had forgotten what they were talking about. "Sorry for what?"

Wayne gave her a wry grin, like she'd nailed the lightning round and won the grand prize. He reached for the pencil cup again. "How old are you now? Twelve?"

"Thirteen."

Wayne ran his hand over his cue-ball head. "Anybody give you trouble at school anymore?"

Gina shook her head. The Dio body allowed her to pass for eighteen. The last time anyone tried to mess with her was in fourth grade when Terry Valli taped a sign reading WIDE LOAD on her back. Terry spent a week in the ICU and eventually transferred out of the district. Gina had gotten suspended for a week. She would have done it all over again.

"I got a job for you." Uncle Wayne tapped the pencil on the desk. "I think you'd do real good with it. And it would help you out."

"What kind of job?"

"Nothing you can't handle." He picked up a notepad and scribbled on it. "Need you to go to this address." He ripped off the small spiral-edged sheet and handed it to her. "Guy lives there by the name of Dobish. He's got some money for me."

Gina took the scrap of paper. It was an address on Hirsch Street up in Humboldt Park. A part of town her uncles only ever mentioned in mean jokes. "Does he know I'm coming?"

"No, and that's why you're going and not me." He pointed to himself and made a face. "He sees this standing outside his door, he's not liable to invite me in."

Gina smiled and put the scrap of paper in her pocket. "What if he doesn't have the money?"

"He'll have it," Wayne said. "You'll see. Some of these guys, I swear." He leaned back in the chair. "Act like we put a gun to their heads, made them place those bets."

Gina stared at the ceramic kids. Their blank, cheerful eyes. Maybe it would be fun to go on a cruise with a bunch of goats, and maybe it wouldn't. Either way, there would be a lot of goat shit to clean up. If you didn't understand that going in, you were a moron.

"Ten percent of whatever you get is yours," Wayne said. "Got it?"

Dobish was the only Ukrainian name on the list of six doorbells. The rest were all Puerto Rican. Gina pressed her finger into the grimy buzzer and heard an echo in the bowels of the grim brownstone block. Through the glass door she could see a tiny foyer with a bay of dented metal mailboxes.

No answer. Gina swirled her bat in tiny circles. She thought she'd get some stares on the Damen Avenue bus, looking like she was headed for softball practice in the middle of a blizzard, but nobody gave her a second glance. She was invisible. She should have been used to it by now.

She buzzed again and this time the intercom snapped to life. A baby's wail burst through it, mid-breath. It sounded like it had been going on for a long time. "Shut it!" a man's fuzzy voice shouted somewhere far off. The baby wailed louder. "Hello?" The voice was suddenly close.

Gina stared at the intercom grille. The baby had caught her off guard.

"*Hello?* Who's out there?"

"I got your mail," Gina said, staring at the packages and flyers littering the entryway floor. "The mailman messed up. I live down the street."

A shuffling noise, and the baby stopped crying with a sharp hiccup. Gina flinched.

"Leave it inside." The buzzer gave an angry snort. Gina scrabbled the door open and slipped inside. Her bat got stuck and the door smashed down on it. She yanked the bat loose and lurched up the stairs.

Two kids were playing in the dark stairwell, tossing cards down on the steps and slapping at them. They stopped and watched her climb toward them but didn't move apart. She had to push through them, scattering the cards. The boy, older, said something in rapid-fire Spanish, and the girl laughed. Gina ignored them.

By the time she reached Dobish's door the baby was shrieking again. *Knock knock*. She could hear a TV blasting out audience cheers and electronic dings. There was an exasperated sigh and the TV noise fell quiet.

The voice from the intercom called something out but she couldn't hear it over the baby's wailing.

"Hi, me again," Gina said. "I dropped off your mail. Listen mister, I really got to use the bathroom. Can I come in for a sec?"

A snort, like he couldn't believe the balls on her. "S'ain't the YMCA. Get lost." Slow, thick whisky words. Good, Gina thought. If he'd had a few, he wouldn't pick too hard at her bullshit story.

The baby's power-drill keening finally gave out. Gina pressed her ear to the door. "Come on, mister. I'll be in and out. It's an *emergency*." She put a whine on the last word, like a spin on a ball headed for home plate. She knew if there was anything a drunk asshole hated, it was a woman *flapping her gums*.

"Jesus, Mary and ..." He drifted off, like he forgot the rest of the lineup. She heard shuffling sounds. Bingo. He'd probably figured out he'd get rid of her faster if he let her in.

The deadbolt slid aside and a watery eye appeared on the other side of the chain. Boozy vapor wafted through the door, followed by other smells. Old food and something earthy and rotten.

"Mi casa es su casa." He unlocked the chain and stepped back with a mocking bow. He was a short guy with thinning hair he kept running his hands through, like he was trying to coax it to grow back.

Gina squinted into the hot, dim room. The only furniture was a cockeyed coffee table and a couple of metal folding chairs that looked like they'd been lifted from a school auditorium. Stained carpeting, bald where the couch used to be. A surprisingly large TV was showing "The Price is Right." The show intro flashed onto the screen, framed in winking golden lights. Dobish was already staring back at it, a bright window into a world of crisp dollar bills and beautiful people.

Gina pushed past Dobish and found the worn bassinet in a corner. The baby inside was too big for it, his little feet pushing against the walls. Wearing dirty fleece pajamas too hot for the room—no wonder he was howling. Gina unzipped him to find a smelly, bulging diaper. No marks on his doughy body, but he didn't exactly look healthy, either. He sniffled and moved his tiny hands like an upended turtle. An overflowing diaper pail stood nearby.

"When was the last time you changed this kid's diaper?" Gina said.

"What are you, the Pampers police?" Dobish was already sitting back down in the metal chair. On TV, a woman with crimped blonde hair was guessing how much a white grand piano cost. Her nose wrinkled with concentration. Dobish leaned forward, watching. Gina would be surprised if he knew what a piano was used for, but he was staring at it with rats' eyes, glossy and bottomless. On the cracked wall above him, a piece of latch-hook art hung in a frame: block letters someone had worked hard to get almost straight. BLESS THIS MESS.

"Where's your wife?" Gina asked.

"Working." Dobish aimed the remote at the TV and looked up at Gina. "What? It's modern times." He smirked. "I'm Mr. Mom."

Gina's fingers closed tighter around the bat. Stupid asshole thought she was calling him a pussy for doing *women's work*. Which, beneath him or not, he still couldn't handle. Gina wondered what Mrs. Dobish would do when she got home from working all day so this douche bag could sit in front of the TV with dollar signs dancing in his eyes. Fran's face swam up in Gina's mind. The prim look she got when she didn't like what was happening but didn't think she could stop it. The fat dago cunt look.

"I'm here from Wayne Dio," Gina said quietly from behind clenched teeth. "You got his money." She was careful not to make it a question or a request.

Dobish didn't look at her but he sat up straighter. Keeping cool, Gina thought, while he figured out how to play this.

"I don't have it." He thumbed a button and the TV got louder. Bob Barker waved his arm and the screen whirled to commercial through a star-shaped video effect. Dobish didn't move. "I'll have it next week."

He was lying. Watching her dad had taught Gina all the tells, all the shitty little ploys these guys pulled to see how far they could go, how much they could get away with. Rules were for chumps. These guys were too smart for rules. Too smart to get caught. And when they did get caught, it was everyone's fault but theirs.

"You have it now," Gina said. "I'll take it now."

A sly wrinkle bent Dobish's lips. "How about I give it to you in peanut butter sandwiches?"

Gina took two steps across the filthy carpet, raised the bat and cracked Dobish across the face. A dull thump of wood on bone. The chair fell sideways, spilling him onto his side. Dobish gasped, eyes spinning, and clapped his hand to his purpling temple. Then he opened his mouth and began to howl. The baby joined him.

"Get up," Gina raised her voice. "Go get the money." The two voices rose around her in jagged leaps and whorls. "And a clean diaper." She was shouting now.

Cigarette smoke and coffee. Their heavy mix hanging in the air every morning was how Gina knew she was awake. She rolled over in bed and stretched. Jenny's bed was empty. Jake must be having a good day. He must have taken Kyle and Jenny to the park to throw the ball around. Gina was rarely invited, and that was okay. She relaxed, soaking up the silence. Maybe she and Fran could have breakfast together without Fran having to get up every two seconds. They'd eat at the tiny table and Fran would stare out the window facing the scraggly side yard, smiling at it like it was the ocean. It was okay with Gina if they didn't talk. They just had to make sure to clean up before Jake got home. Jake hated a mess.

Gina got dressed, brushed her teeth in the tiny bathroom, and went into the kitchen. Fran was at the table, cigarette in hand. Her other hand was white-knuckling the handle of a chipped coffee cup. Ash teetered on the end of the cigarette, over the coffee.

The only other thing on the table was Gina's money, spread out in a neat fan.

Prize money, Gina thought wildly, and "The Price is Right" flashed through her mind again. She had hidden the money in a tampon box under the bed, in the room she shared with Jenny. It was the only place she knew Jake would never look when he ransacked the house for cash. How did she miss Fran rooting under her bed while she slept? A chill shook her: did Jake already know? He'd take the money and there wouldn't be a damn thing she could do about it.

Fran was still wearing her bar makeup from the night before, creased in dark streaks around her eyes. She stared at Gina and shook her head. *Jesus*, her face said. *Not one more thing.* Gina felt sick. She'd just wanted to make things better. She had lain awake all night thinking of ways to use the money without anyone—especially Jake—noticing. Slip a few dollars here and there into Fran's wallet? Buy those nasty onion-flavored chips Fran liked and pretend they were in the pantry all along? Stupid. Every idea she had was stupid. She was still puzzling things out when her thoughts slid sideways and winked out.

The ash fell from Fran's cigarette and scattered on the table, missing the coffee by an inch. "Where did you steal it from?" she asked.

Gina looked up sharply. Her face blazed. *Oh sure,* she thought. *Now stealing is wrong?* "I didn't steal it," she said. "*I'm* not a thief." She knew she'd get in trouble but she couldn't stop herself from punching that first word. *Never going to be a goddamn dirty scumbag thief. Ever.* That one had topped the list for years.

Fran eased up from the table. She came toward Gina and leaned in, so close Gina could smell the smoke and coffee on her breath. Gina turned away, waiting for the sharp sting against her cheek.

But Fran didn't hit her. "You watch yourself, Regina Brown," she said softly. Gina blanched and squeezed her lips together. The name—*his* name—was worse than a slap. The minute she turned eighteen—the second—she'd march down to city hall and change her last name back to Dio.

"I'm in your room looking around for a tampon," Fran said. "And instead I find *this*." She motioned back to the table. Dobish had forked over the two grand he owed, and, true to his word, Uncle Wayne had stripped ten sweaty, crumpled twenties out of the pile and handed them back to Gina.

Gina's mind raced. Fran would freak if she knew where the money had come from. Gina would be in deep shit, and so would Wayne.

"I'm waiting, Regina." Fran clearly couldn't even muster up her principal voice. She just sounded tired. "Your father will be home any minute. You want to explain this to him too?"

Gina lowered her head. *Never lie to Mom.* One of the oldest Greatest Hits there was. "Uncle Wayne," she said. "I got it from Uncle Wayne."

Fran's face changed. The tired look disappeared and rage bloomed in its place. Gina closed her eyes and waited. She heard Fran stalk to the front closet.

"Get your coat, Gina." Fran already had her coat on. She took Gina's down from the hanger and tossed it at her.

They walked the two blocks down to the corner to Josie's, Fran marching ahead, Gina stumbling along behind her. Gina knew she was hosed. This, in Fran's mind, was worse than stealing. This was *charity*. Gina wondered which Fran would think was worse: that her own family thought she was a miserable fuckup or that her daughter had turned a guy's face to hamburger for two hundred bucks. *He brought it on himself,* Gina thought sulkily, kicking at a clump of dirty snow. *Nobody held a gun to his head.*

At ten in the morning, Josie's was closed, so they knocked on the side window and waited for Wayne to come out. He was wearing tiny round reading glasses that reflected the morning light and made him look like he had no eyes. He gave Fran a kiss on the cheek and invited them back into his office. If he knew things had gone kablooey, he didn't show it.

Today a mechanical calculator sat in the center of the big desk, surrounded by mountains of receipts. Wayne dragged a second chair up to the one where Gina had sat the day before, and motioned for the two of them to sit.

"We're not staying." Fran fumbled in her purse. "We just came to give this back." She thrust the cash at him in a crumpled fistful. "We don't want it. We don't need it." Her lips were stretched thin. In her puffy coat she looked like one of those South American birds that stuck up its feathers to look dangerous.

Wayne looked at the money, then at Fran. "Is that right?" He sat down behind the desk.

"I'm done, Wayne," Fran said. "I have had just about enough of this pity bullshit."

Wayne raised his eyebrows but didn't interrupt her.

"That's right." Fran's nose was running from the cold. She wiped at it angrily. "I know what you and Joey and all them say about us when I'm not around, but you know what?" She counted on her fingers. "I just picked up an extra shift at the bar. Jake's been out of, you know, out of trouble for a long time now. And he's building up seniority. Any day now they're going to start giving him the good routes. Any day."

Gina screwed her eyes shut and wished she could do the same for her ears. *Stop it, stop it, stop it.*

But Fran didn't stop. "Things are turning around for us. Okay? So can all of you just mind your own goddamned business for once?" Her voice rose, then gave out in a high-pitched squeak.

Wayne took off his glasses and set them on the desk. "Now, hold on a second. Back up." He picked up money. "What do you think this is, a handout?" He motioned to Gina. "She earned that money, fair and square. This ain't no soup kitchen."

"Earned it?" Fran looked at Gina. "Doing what?"

Gina shrank in her stifling coat but Wayne didn't bat an eyelash. "Helping out with the room."

"Helping out with the ..." Fran swept her hand across her forehead and sank into the chair. "Wayne. She is thirteen years old."

"Yeah, I know how old she is, Fran." Wayne's tone sharpened. "She's not a kid anymore." For the first time since they'd walked in, he looked at Gina. "She's tough and she's smart. She can handle herself." He leaned back in the chair. "If I were you, I'd get the fuck out of her way."

Fran thrust her chin up. "She wasn't serving drinks, was she?"

"What are you, nuts?" Wayne said. "She just, you know, ran some errands, cleaned up. That kind of thing." Gina felt a noise trying to burst from her throat, either a laugh or a sob. *It's not really lying,* she thought. *Is it?*

"Look. Fran." Wayne's tone softened. "You got a real special kid here. She earned this money and she's keeping it. She wants to share it with you, that's up to her, but this ain't about you." He stood up and handed the stack of bills to Gina. Fran followed it with her eyes.

Gina folded the money into her coat. "Thanks," she mumbled. Fran was still looking at Gina's pocket, where the money had gone. "Are you going to tell Dad?" Gina asked her.

When Fran looked up her face was very still. "You heard your uncle," she said in a flat tone. "It's your money. You want to tell your dad about it, you tell him. I'm not going to."

Gina's heart skipped a beat. She searched her mom's face, but it was blank. Like Fran was afraid the face she wore every day was about to slip and show everyone what was underneath.

"Now." Wayne sat back down. "You coming back tomorrow after school, or what? I got more stuff needs doing."

Fran was smiling now, nodding at Gina. The old Fran, normal Fran. That creepy pleading mask was gone. *I knew it,* she would tell Gina on the way home. *I knew things were about to turn around. You just have to have patience. Have faith.* When they got home she would offer to make pancakes, and now they could buy all the eggs in the goddamn store if they wanted to. Gina would even run out and get them, she didn't mind. Isn't that what Jake was always telling her, standing in the doorway of her room late at night, blocking the light? That she needed to be more responsible?

"I'll be back tomorrow," Gina said to Uncle Wayne. She would be responsible. She would be responsible and she would like it.

FLEECE NAVIDAD

A You-Solve-It by Stacy Woodson

Postmaster Mabel Fitzgibbon sat in the driver's seat of an antique mail truck, engine idling, while she waited for Pottsville's Christmas Day Parade to begin. Her job was to lead the floats in the staging area down Main Street once the judging for the parade's best float competition was finished. Hal's Hardware store sponsored the contest, and the winning float would be featured in a television commercial promoting his store. Yesterday, during preliminary judging, Hal had picked two finalists, both featuring Miss Christmas pageant contestants.

The Pottsville Theatre was the first finalist. They had recreated a scene from their production of *A Christmas Carol.* Set pieces and actors dressed in period costumes filled the float. Pageant contestant and aspiring actress, Ruthanne Mosby, played the ghost of Christmas past. The float that belonged to the Pottsville Carolers had also made the cut and featured Ruthanne's beauty queen rival, Dixie Lynn Taylor, singing *White Christmas.*

Mabel was secretly glad the Post Office didn't have a float this year. She hated public speaking, and the thought of being in a commercial terrified her, a spotlight Ruthanne and Dixie Lynn would likely relish. Mabel was also glad the parade was delayed because it gave her time to work on the daily crossword puzzle.

The latest stumper—17 across. Six empty boxes. The clue: Santa's vehicle. Sleigh was a natural fit, but it didn't work with her other answers—answers she knew were correct. She considered synonyms. Sled was too short, toboggan too long.

Someone knocked on Mabel's window.

She reluctantly looked up from her puzzle. Hal stood there with Bethany, a reporter from *Sunrise with Pottsville.* Bethany's teased out hair reminded Mabel of spiral perms, shoulder pads, and leg warmers—all head-shaking fashion choices of the 1980s.

Bethany's cameraman was with her, too. Seeing the camera and the wide lens made Mabel's palms sweat. She should have worn make-up, at least a touch of lipstick. She thought about her cosmetic bag at home tucked under her bathroom sink gathering dust. She smoothed her hair and prayed that they wouldn't want an interview.

But the cameraman placed his camera on the ground, his attention on a piece of candy cane stuck to the frayed cuff of his wool jacket—a pink stain already bleeding through.

Relieved he was distracted, Mabel finally cranked down the window. "Morning, Hal. Finally, pick a winner?"

Before Hal could answer, Bethany interrupted, "You need to decide, Hal. We go live in ten minutes and need time to set-up in front of the blue-ribbon float."

"I'm aware of the timeline, Bethany," Hal said, an edge to his voice.

"It's starting to drizzle." Bethany pressed, touching her hair.

"What does that have to do with anything?" Hal asked.

Bethany's eyes narrowed.

The cameraman said, "I think what Bethany is trying to say is that it's Smiley Joe Riley's last day as the anchor for the morning show, and she wants things to move as smoothly as possible."

"I can't believe he's retiring," Hal said. "He's been an anchor on that show since I was in elementary school."

"He's an icon," Bethany agreed.

"Any news on his replacement?" Hal asked.

"Not yet."

"Well, he's going to be missed."

Bethany glanced at her watch. "We go live in eight, Hal."

"Just give me two minutes, okay?"

She nodded, reluctantly.

Hal stepped closer to the postal truck and whispered to Mabel. "I can't pick a float. Mind walking the line with me?"

Mabel flushed, pleased Hal valued her opinion. She killed the engine, tucked her puzzle under the visor, and climbed out of the truck.

"Any luck with 17 across?" Hal asked, as they made their way down the line of floats to the finalists. He enjoyed puzzles like Mabel and had recently joined the Pottsville Puzzlers where she was a member.

"I have no idea," Mabel admitted.

"It stumped me, too," Hal said as they approached the Christmas Carol float. "Sleigh seemed like such a natural—" But Mabel didn't hear the rest. Hal's voice was drowned out by Ruthanne's.

"I can't believe you did this," Ruthanne yelled. She flung her bonnet back and pointed her gray hand warming muff at Dixie Lynn like it was a scolding finger. "You've dealt some low blows in the past, Dixie Lynn, but this one takes the cake."

Dixie Lynn folded her arms. She stood on the Caroler's float next to Ruthanne's, her fur-lined dress pooling around her. "I don't know what you're talking about."

And neither did Mabel, until she was close enough to see Pottsville Theatre's float. Nothing remained of the re-imagined Yorkshire town of Malton except for piles of paint colored plywood that littered the back of the flatbed. A sledgehammer, tufts of fleece stuck to the handle, was discarded among the debris—likely the weapon that inflicted the damage.

Ruthanne continued still enraged. "You knew that Hal's commercial was a big break, a big break we both needed. And when it looked like my float was going to win—"

"Vandalism runs rampant at Pottsville's Christmas Parade," Bethany's excited voice carried over the commotion. She had positioned herself for a stand-up right in front of the damaged float while her cameraman panned over the pieces of wood and debris.

"Who would do such a thing?" Hal shook his head. "We need to call the sheriff."

Mabel looked at the float and then back at Bethany and her cameraman. She agreed with Hal. They needed to make the call. Especially, since she knew the vandal's identity and now, blessedly, the answer to 17 across.

Solution in next month's issue ...

SOLUTION TO NOVEMBER'S YOU-SOLVE-IT

Which Casino? By Arthur Vidro

This gang is big on palindromes. They use the names Bob, Otto, Eve, and Hannah. They eat at Mom & Dad's. They order burgers on naan bread. So the casino they would choose is Harrah's.

Manufactured by Amazon.ca
Bolton, ON

51848461R00052